After almost 30 years in home improvement management and at the pinnacle of his profession, Dan fulfilled a lifetime goal and switched careers to become a middle school teacher. Ten years of teaching was a wonderful experience for Dan, and mentoring young, diverse students was very rewarding.

Dan has a BLS in History from the University of Mary Washington in Fredericksburg, Virginia, and an MBA from Emory University in Atlanta, Georgia. Now retired, Dan lives in Richmond, Virginia, with his wife of 36 years, Sue.

This book is dedicated to my wife, Sue, who patiently listened to my daily stories about teaching, and to all of the students who worked hard, had fun, and brought energy and joy to my classroom. I would also like to recognize all educators, past and present, for your underappreciated role in shaping America's youth and success.

Daniel Kneip

PUBLIC EDUCATION: SPENDING LESS, ACHIEVING LESSER

AUSTIN MACAULEY PUBLISHERS™
LONDON • CAMBRIDGE • NEW YORK • SHARJAH

Copyright © Daniel Kneip (2021)

All rights reserved. No part of this publication may be reproduced, distributed, or transmitted in any form or by any means, including photocopying, recording, or other electronic or mechanical methods, without the prior written permission of the publisher, except in the case of brief quotations embodied in critical reviews and certain other noncommercial uses permitted by copyright law. For permission requests, write to the publisher.

Any person who commits any unauthorized act in relation to this publication may be liable to criminal prosecution and civil claims for damages.

This is a work of fiction. Names, characters, businesses, places, events, locales, and incidents are either the products of the author's imagination or used in a fictitious manner. Any resemblance to actual persons, living or dead, or actual events is purely coincidental.

Ordering Information
Quantity sales: Special discounts are available on quantity purchases by corporations, associations, and others. For details, contact the publisher at the address below.

Publisher's Cataloging-in-Publication data
Kneip, Daniel
Public Education: Spending Less, Achieving Lesser

ISBN 9781647504038 (Paperback)
ISBN 9781647504021 (Hardback)
ISBN 9781647504045 (ePub e-book)

Library of Congress Control Number: 2021904085

www.austinmacauley.com/us

First Published (2021)
Austin Macauley Publishers LLC
40 Wall Street, 33rd Floor, Suite 3302
New York, NY 10005
USA

mail-usa@austinmacauley.com
+1 (646) 5125767

As a work of fiction, it is difficult to acknowledge individuals, but I would like to recognize the students and faculty at Battlefield Middle School in Fredericksburg, Virginia, as the inspiration for this book. I also want to mention my mentor and friend, Dr. Sheila Smith, Ed.D., who took personal interest to make sure I succeeded as a career switcher. Lastly, a big thank you to my fellow warrior, Tony Fatiga. I miss our years of early morning comradery as we prepared to teach and accommodate our students each day.

Synopsis

An eighth-grader, Cecelia, who is also an office aide, enters the classroom with a note to bring a student to guidance with her.

"Do you have a subpoena?" the teacher jokes.

"No!" she replies. "I'm a *girl!*"

Perhaps the most unusual collection of educators ever assembled in one middle school. And that's saying a lot! Ed Knudknickovich, a comedy writer who switches careers to teach history; Kilo Jones, the eccentric science teacher whose name is *not* based on the metric system; Rhoda Atlas, the vindictive and intimidating school nurse; by-the-book Vice Principal Derry, labeled 'Derry Queen the King of Mean' by the students; Principal Cutty, who is charged with peacefully fusing faculty, students, and parents; peculiar Guy White, a teacher and would-be inventor who might just be the sanest of them all; and a supporting cast that includes Logan Click, an introspective sixth-grader still dealing with the loss of her father; savvy classmate Andre Martinez, who looks and acts 18; and his best friend Fowler, who is smart but naive.

Everyone has memories, good and bad, of their school years. With 900 kids and adults spending 180 days inside

the same four walls, anything can happen, and as you recall,
it usually does…

Prologue

Edward Knudknickovich, forty, tall, lean, and shaggy-haired, looks out through the glass wall of the room dubbed 'The Fishbowl.' Years of stand-up comedy culminating in a decade of writing for *The Daily Show with Jon Stewart* in New York City has been a great ride, but his frat-like lifestyle is getting old. Ed's frustration with the younger group of writers creates an inner conflict of stay or go; their usual juvenile behavior, things like practical jokes and stacking coffee cups into towers is a constant annoyance. He's been thinking of leaving, but what's next? Just then Ed is hit in the back of the head with a balled-up sheet of paper.

"Hey ka-nud-nuts," one of the other writers says. "Are we keeping you awake?"

"I told you not to call me that," Ed responds.

"Everybody does."

Ed turns away. Annoyed, Ed's pensive face reflects his growing disillusionment. His cell phone vibrates. It shows an incoming call from his sister, Anita.

"Hey. What? When? Where are you? Let me get out of here and call you back. OK."

Before Ed reaches the glass door, it swings open. One of the show's producers barges in.

"Well," the producer says, "We knew it was coming. Jon just made it official. He announced he's leaving in August."

There is a buzz of questions and comments as the employee's futures are suddenly unclear.

"Hold on. We're meeting at 3:00," the producer says. "You'll get all the answers."

Ed, distracted, leaves the room and re-dials his sister.

"It's me. I can't believe it! He wasn't even sick, was he? What happened? Yeah, I'm coming down. I need to get out of here anyway. I might stay for a while. I'll explain. It's not important now. Give me some time so I can rent a car and hit the Turnpike. I'll call from the road."

Ed looks upset as he walks down the hallway in a hurry, ignoring his coworkers. It seems the catalyst for his decision to quit might have been made for him. But now what?

Chapter One

Anita Gold, Ed's forty-eight-year-old sister, appearing fatigued and exhausted, reluctantly discusses her husband's funeral held earlier that day as she sits at her kitchen counter with Ed. All of the visitors have finally left. Anita's eyes are still red.

"I can't believe Harold's gone," Ed says as they share coffee.

"And there's no history of heart problems in his family?"

"No, that's why it was such a surprise," Anita says while holding back tears.

"I can't believe in 2015 they can't detect heart problems before they hit. What are you going to do now?"

"What do you mean?"

"Well, I mean, you aren't going back to work, are you?"

"Why wouldn't I?" Anita asks.

"I don't know. I'm just talking. It seems like being a high school principal must be very stressful, something you don't need more of right now."

"Yes, but it took me a long time to work my way up, plus I enjoy it. Since it is summer, it's been a little easier to take some time off."

"Are you going to change your last name back?"

"I don't know. I haven't thought about some of those things yet. I've been Anita Gold longer than Anita Knudknickovich. Besides, would *you* want our last name back?"

"Good point. I just wish I lived closer. I feel bad and want to help however I can," Ed says sincerely.

"You've been great. I have a pretty good support system around me since I've lived here for so long. I'm going to keep the house, maybe downsize in a few years."

"So, you're staying in Po-dunk Virginia?"

"It's called Farmwood, but you know that. And why would I leave?"

"I don't know," Ed says, "Being alone is certainly not what you planned for your golden years. I'm just worried about you. You tend to hold your emotions in pretty well, like me. It must be a family thing."

"Um, I'm not that old and I've been here for so many years, away from the city. Let's talk later. I'm exhausted, wiped out from the last week. I could use a nap."

"Before you go, I have some news."

"Oh?"

"I kind of, pretty much, quit my job."

"You did? What happened? Is it because Jon's leaving?"

"You heard?" Ed asks. He gets up and rinses his coffee cup in the sink.

"Yes, we have news and cable here, just so you know. So?"

"It's been frustrating for a year or so." Ed was glad to have someone to talk to about it.

"The writing staff keeps getting younger. Millennials and generation x-ers, and I keep getting older. And you know how it's always been. You're only as good as your last joke. I made some good money, got my name on a couple writing Emmys, but I feel very restless. I always wanted to be head-writer but never got it. I need a change, but I have no idea what I want to do next. Something where you feel a sense of accomplishment, and maybe less stressful than banging out a show four nights a week."

"Become a teacher," Anita replies.

"What? Where did *that* come from?"

"I've been thinking about it," Anita says. "Mom was a teacher, and I worked my way up to principal. And trust me, you won't miss the city. You could live here with me, at least to get started."

"I hated school. Why would I want to be a teacher?"

"Listen, it can be an incredibly rewarding career. Sure, there are burned-out teachers that don't care but it's a small percentage. Helping kids learn, watching them 'get it,' there's nothing better."

"Well," Ed replies, "I *have* mentored a lot of younger writers. In fact, they usually make me the new person's 'buddy' for the first sixty days to get them acclimated and make sure they succeed. And it is, or was, one of the best parts of the job."

"Think about it. Let's talk some more later."

That evening Anita walks into the living room and finds her brother enjoying a beer.

"Did you sleep?" Ed asks.

"Not really. I just want this day to be done. What are you writing?"

Ed has a yellow pad and pen, writing notes. With her husband gone, Anita realizes how much she misses her brother. She wishes he would stay but knows him well, and subtly always works best.

"Will you at least think about what we talked about? Being a teacher can be fun."

"I have, and I am. I'm making a list, but I didn't put 'fun' on it. And leaving New York after all these years for rural Virginia. Talk about a fish out of water."

"Here, help me clean out your room while we talk."

Anita leads Ed into a spare bedroom in the medium-sized house, and they work together to move things collected over the years.

"Teaching can be fun. You know how you were always the class clown? I mean, you'd get in trouble once in a while, but you were *entertaining*. And that's how you ended up in comedy. You even did stand-up for a while."

"And?"

"And entertaining, keeping kids interested, that's huge. You'd be great at it. And you always liked history. Why not teach it?"

"You make it sound possible. I promise to keep thinking about it. I was making great money, so one of the things I wrote on my list is that I can probably *afford* to be a teacher. Does it still pay minimum wage?"

Ed gets another beer from the kitchen.

"Haha. I know you banked a lot. And yes, this would be a huge pay cut, but that's not the reward anyway."

"I know," Ed says. "And maybe it is time for me to get out of New York City. But becoming a teacher? Here? That sounds like a lot of work. Can you just write me a note making me a teacher or something? I mean, I have no idea how to get started. I really don't want to go back to school to be a teacher."

"Now there's a dose of irony. You don't want to go to school to be a teacher!"

"Yeah, and that thing you were talking about before, that transformer thing."

"Career Transition Training. It's not a 'thing.'"

"Whatever. How does it work again? Let me unpack some of my stuff while we talk."

Ed takes a suitcase and two black garbage bags full of his clothes and begins to stuff them into an empty dresser.

"Well," Anita continues. "Because this is such a rural area, it's hard to get any professionals to practice here. Good luck finding a doctor or a lawyer."

"This is not helping."

"And, it's hard to recruit teachers as well. Plus, there are no unions in Virginia, so the pay is terrible. If you just graduated from college with forty or fifty thousand dollars or more in student loans this is the *last* place you want to work."

"You're not in charge of recruiting, are you?"

"Haha. I'm just being honest. So, the county and state started a Career Transition Training program to convert people who are interested in a second career as a teacher. I was involved in the entire process; the training and placement, and I've hired a few myself."

"And you think I could do it?"

"I *know* you can do it," Anita says confidently. "And you are already qualified. You have a bachelor's degree and solid work history, which are two of the mandatory requirements. You could stay here and take the classes every Friday night and all-day Saturday for five months. That gets you a one-year provisional license. You'll get a job. And I can help."

"But my experience is writing jokes. For someone else."

"Well, guess what? Like I said, half of teaching is keeping the kids engaged and interested. That's the hardest part. And you can certainly do that."

"I guess. And as long as you can still spank the kids, curse at the parents, and hit on the mothers, I'm in!"

Anita stares him down. Ed continues his skepticism, having never liked school, as well as having several teachers tell him he would never amount to anything. Done in the bedroom, they move back into the living room.

Anita continues her pitch.

"You know what they say are the three best reasons to be a teacher?"

"Wow, there's that many?"

"June, July, and August, wise guy. And we are the last of the Knudknickovichs. Especially now. It would be great to have you close. Wouldn't it be nice to see your sister more often? I can't tell you how important it is to me that we spend more time together than we have. We are it for family. I can help you as a teacher and you can help me as a widow starting over."

"I definitely need a change, something with a sense of satisfaction. I remember all of my teachers, both good and bad, so you're right, I could make an impact on kids. And I do miss you, a lot. I'll need some help, but I might just try this…"

"There's a new Career Transition Training program in a couple of months for new hires next year, so don't wait too long to decide."

Ed plops down on the living room couch and grabs the remote. Anita smiles as she feels she is making progress, but sadness about losing Harold creeps in again.

His decision made, it takes some time for Ed to rent a small U-Haul truck, double-park it and get friends to help load the few things he is keeping from his New York City apartment. It is a stressful time for Ed. As he drives, his mind stays flummoxed: making it to Anita's house; attending Transition Training classes in a month; hoping to get hired; and beginning a new school year. He shifts between fear and opportunity. At least worrying makes the drive into central Virginia go faster.

Ed stays with Anita the entire five months of the Career Transition Training. Anita enjoys the company and renewing her relationship with her brother, especially after being unexpectantly alone now. She is helpful, giving Ed a list of old interview questions, for example, and mock interviewing him. Topics like classroom management, how to use a curriculum guide, and dealing with parents, keeps Ed engaged. He is gaining confidence as he takes copious notes from the teachers and counselors grooming the would-be teachers in the program. Even the Superintendent visits to meet the small group and offer encouragement. Ed successfully finishes the training with an appetite to get in a classroom, having exorcised his initial fears.

Now comes the big event. The roundtable interview for a position at the middle school. There is only one opening for a history teacher as math and science teachers are in larger demand. Ed's career is now in the hands of the four people in the conference room.

Ed's hair is shorter, and he is squirming in a suit and tie, an unfamiliar, and uncomfortable, wardrobe. Ed is brought in by the school's office manager, a friendly woman who makes Ed feel at ease, at least temporarily. At the head of the table, introductions begin.

"Come in, Edward. Take a seat. I'm Principal Cutty. Is it Ed or Edward?"

"Ed is fine," he says, sitting in one of the high back chairs.

"Let me introduce the others," Cutty continues in an amiable voice. Cutty appears petite with long, dark hair.

"This is Vice Principal Derry. He oversees sixth grade."

Derry seems very young; much younger than Ed. His crew-cut hair and stiff body language makes Ed think he might be former military. Ed's intuition perks up about Derry, who seems intense and uptight.

"This is Kwaji, our lead guidance counselor. He is also responsible for the sixth grade. You would see a lot of him." A Pacific islander, Kwaji has a very welcoming smile.

"And this fellow is Kilo Jones," Cutty says, nodding toward a bearded man about fifty who seems relaxed and friendly.

"He is a sixth-grade science teacher. We always have a teacher sit in to get their perspective when we interview, and to make sure people will fit our culture."

Ed smiles at everyone as he shakes their hands. He is hiding his insecurity well, although he fears his palm is a little moist from nerves.

Each person has a manila folder in front of them as Derry begins the interview.

"You certainly have an interesting background, Ed. I have two concerns. Your transcripts from NYU seem very, I guess average is the word. And your work history is solid, but teaching is very different than writing jokes. Can you make the transition?" Derry asks.

"That's a very fair question," Ed replies. "On paper I would say I can't compete with experienced teachers, or recent college grads you may interview. But what I'm selling is *potential*. Plus, you know what you are getting. Maturity, work ethic, all the things that are a gamble when hiring a twenty-two-year-old. And you get someone with a willingness to learn and adapt, no baggage so to speak, that more experienced teachers may or may not have."

Principal Cutty says, "I like that answer. I'm fine with potential."

Similar conversations continue as they speak about curriculum, classroom management, and lesson plans, and Ed gives good answers because of the Career Transition Training he attended.

A bit later Cutty says, "I have two final questions. Neither is about academics nor resumes. First, Ed, why do you want to be a teacher?"

Anita had coached him on this one: "*Don't* say 'I always wanted to be a teacher' but speak from the heart."

"Well, you know my sister, Anita, has been in education for twenty-five years or so, and she loves it. I always felt a sense of pride when she would talk about her role in the community. For me, this is not a job. It is a second career. More importantly, I love to learn, as well as share knowledge. I have a history of mentoring and helping new hires. And I remember my middle school years very well, and I am certainly aware of the impact, both good and bad, a teacher can have. I would like to be a role model for today's youth."

"And my last question," Cutty says. "Who is someone you respect, and why?"

"This might sound odd because it's a fictional character, but I would have to say Forrest Gump."

This brings a guffaw from Derry. "That's a new one," Derry says. "What college did you attend again?"

"Go on, please," Cutty says, staring down Derry.

"The reason I admire Forrest Gump is that no matter what situation he was in, he always gave his best. Yes, he kind of floated through life without a clear plan or goal, but hard work and determination brought him success several times. No job was too small or too large. Giving one hundred percent was innate. I respect that. Whether I was staying late or called back in, or rewriting until the jokes were just right, or being the first one in every day, I was always inspired by his work ethic. He pushed, he tried, and he never quit. And since I would be a role model to students, I'd want them to know hard work, effort, and perseverance trumps anything else in life, except education, and is a key to success. I'd like the opportunity to share that with kids who might not have a role model at home. I can see how that would feel very rewarding, something missing from my life.

"I also want to say you would have my one hundred percent commitment. This is a second career; I don't have a third. You'll have my total buy in."

"Great answer," Cutty says.

"And very original." Cutty smiles and says, "By all reports you did very well in the Career Transition Training; lots of participation. And the sixth grade is a wonderful age. Very well. As you know, the school year begins in a few weeks. Any other questions, Kwaji or Kilo?"

Kwaji, who seems preoccupied defers to Kilo Jones.

"Why do some monkeys have big red butts?"

Ed furrows his brow. "Excuse me?"

"I'm kidding. That's the kind of question you'll get from an eleven and twelve-year-old. That's what makes it fun."

"Well then," Cutty says. "We are done. Ed, nice job. If you will please step out for a minute, we are going to debrief and make a decision."

Ed leaves the room and sits in the school office, wondering how busy it would be on a school day with nine-hundred kids and staff roaming around. He senses the interview went well. His serenity is broken when Cutty comes back out.

"We were all impressed with your interview! I'm going to call Betty at human resources in the school board office and ask her to formalize your offer."

"Thank you," Ed says. "That's great!"

Cutty continues. "You'll be joining the sixth-grade teaching team that includes Mr. Jones here, for science; Mr. Larkin, special-ed; Mr. White, English; and Miss Vega, math, who just graduated and will be teaching her first year as well. You'll handle history. I think it's a great team of new and experience. Oh, and because you are both sixth-grade teachers, and your rooms will be next to each other, plus his years of experience, I'm asking Mr. Jones to be your mentor, even though he can be a rascal. He can help guide you in getting things done. How does that sound?"

"That sounds great!" Ed replies.

"And you have a year to pass the state history test for teachers. Any questions?" Cutty concludes.

"No, I'm very excited."

"Oh," Cutty says as if she just recalled something important. "I want to make sure we pronounce your last name correctly."

"It sounds like it's spelled: Most of the Ks are silent so it's Nud-nick-o-vich."

"Very well, Mr. Knudknickovich. You'll get a call from H.R. today or tomorrow. Orientation for new teachers is in two weeks, and then you'll have a week here to get ready before the students arrive on the 5th."

"Thank you so much!"

Kilo Jones follows him out. "I'll see you soon, Ed, *if* that's your real name."

"What?"

"Public education? Public Ed. Too easy. Oh, and watch out for Derry. Not only is he a jackass, but he voted against hiring you. He thinks you'll fail with no experience. He's a by the book control freak, and he's obsessed with state test scores. That's why he would prefer someone with experience. Just an FYI.

"Thanks for the pep talk."

Kilo laughs. "Don't worry. I'll help. See you soon," he says.

That night Ed struggles to sleep. Not really a panic attack, just a lot of 'what ifs?' *Can I do this? What if I fail?*

I quit my job, gave up my apartment. I have to make this work! And I can't let anything, or anyone, stop me.

Chapter Two

Ed attends two days of new teacher orientation, a Thursday and Friday. Time is spent filling out forms, listening to lectures about personal behavior, and representing the school while in public (*don't* get a DUI because you'll be in the newspaper). At the end of the day Ed receives a goody-bag of classroom supplies. He feels ready, anxious to start.

Monday morning comes quickly. There are no students for a week. This is the teacher's time to prepare for the new school year. Except, of course, there were plenty of meetings to attend in the school, covering everything from CPR to how to handle poverty and hunger's detrimental effect on the learning process.

Ed comes in early to start prepping his room, *whatever that means*, he thinks. Luckily, Kilo is an early riser and comes in a few minutes later. Ed is glad Kilo is there and walks into his room to look around.

"So, we finally get to set up our classrooms?" Ed asks, walking around the room and checking out the bulletin boards and other postings. "When did you get all this done?" he asks.

"I've had the same room for fifteen years. I leave most of my stuff hanging up and just do a quick spruce-up."

"Well," Ed replies. "I'm going to get started in my room since we have meetings all week"

"Not yet. We have a couple of hours to complete a chore."

"A chore?"

"Yes. At the beginning of each school year we partner up to make sure the building is ready," Kilo says.

"So, what do we get to do?"

"We get to organize lost and found. I don't know why we don't do it at the *end* of the school year, but who knows."

"Oh, how hard can that be? What is it, a box or a drawer or something?"

"Not exactly. It's everything that kids left in school instead of taking home with them."

The pair walk to a door on the other side of the school and open it. It looks like a large room, but it's fairly dark. Kilo flips a light switch to 'on,' but nothing happens.

"What is that mountain back there?" Ed asks, struggling to make it out.

"You'll see. Let me find the right switch."

"Oh, my God!" Ed exclaims. "That's the biggest pile of clothes I have ever seen! It's taller than us!"

"We call it 'NIKE Mountain.' This is where all the shirts and sweatshirts and shoes and backpacks and who knows what else ends up."

"But, but..." Ed stutters. "There has to be ten years' worth of stuff in here!"

"Nope. Just last year."

"How's that possible? There must be a thousand kids walking around naked! How do you leave your *shoes* here?"

"It's a mystery," Kilo admits.

"All I know is we have to sort it into piles on the tables so the kids can claim it the first day, or we give it to a church. One side boys, one side girls. The middle pile means can't tell. Then by shirts, sweatshirts, shoes, socks, and underwear."

"OK. This has to be a joke. Haha. I mean, look at all this stuff. It looks like a Hollister store exploded!"

"I just remembered I forgot my gloves," Kilo replies.

"Gloves?"

"Yeah. Some of this stuff is pretty nasty. I even found a snake in here one year. It was dead from the smell."

"The smell?"

"You'll see. And watch for bugs."

"Bugs?" Ed asks.

"You'll see. Mostly lice and bedbugs. Put that stuff in a separate pile."

"I don't feel good," Ed says.

"Well, if you are going to throw up, do it over there. That's where the puked-on clothes go."

Kilo starts sorting and Ed reluctantly starts helping.

"Hey," Kilo says. "Let me ask you a question while we sort this junk."

"Shoot."

"Why are you here?"

"*Here,* or here. What do you mean?"

"Here. You've had a pretty exciting life from what I heard in your interview. This is a pretty big change for you. Aren't there other things you could be doing?"

"OK. You got me. Would you believe it is part of a plea bargain? How about for the money? Maybe witness protection?"

"Don't forget I know a lot about you, Mr. Manhattan-man."

"OK, real story."

Kilo and Ed stop for a minute and Kilo sits down on the floor.

"Well, I had a great run in Manhattan. Apartment, a fun job in TV, met all kinds of celebrities. But after years and years, I just got burned out. I needed a change. Then the perfect storm hit when Anita's husband died and Jon Stewart announced he was leaving, so I figured now or never, and I bailed. I had been thinking about leaving. It just wasn't fun anymore. It was Anita's idea for me to move here and teach."

"Pretty bold."

"No kidding. And it has to work. I have some money saved, but if this is Plan B, there is no Plan C. I'm serious. I just spent almost a year getting this far. This *has* to work."

They get back to sorting as their conversation continues.

"My turn for a question," says Ed. "I'm kind of naive on this whole public education thing."

"You came to the right place."

"I mean there are all these rules, and all this paperwork, too. I just never paid attention to this whole debate about education. Anita and I grew up in New York City, so school was like an episode of *Survivor.*"

They continue sorting and stacking clothes, with an occasional gag.

"But here you can't vote anybody off," Kilo says.

"You can't pick your family or your students, I always say."

"Yeah, what was that thing called? 'No Child Left Under the Bus?' I mean, I never heard of core-curriculum, funding issues, and test scores, except when Anita would talk about it once in a while. I just paid my taxes and figured they must have a better plan from when I was in school."

"Nope. Same plan, probably worse. Let me show you my business card."

Kilo reaches for his wallet.

"I didn't know we get business cards," Ed states.

"We don't. I had these made. I've been doing this for so long, and it comes in handy for teacher discounts and stuff. Here you go. Have one."

Ed takes the card. "Having a card makes sense. Let's see. *Kilo Jones. Public School Teacher. We are Spending Less and Achieving Lesser.* This is great! You really hand these out?"

"Sure. What could happen? I don't have the school name on it, and I don't think I've ever had anyone disagree."

"Wow, that's *crazy* bold! But 'lesser' is not a word."

"That's the point. And the truth. The Great Recession was the latest reason to gut school budgets, and all these years later we are still spending less or the same as in 2007. The students are the ones suffering. Allow me to explain the unexplainable. Or at least try."

The two men get comfortable.

"So," Kilo starts, "in Virginia, each county is responsible for the school system. But they rely on the *state* for a lot of the money. And the state relies on the *federal government* for a lot of the money. And both want rules and control in exchange.

"In the old days, a teacher's classroom was their fiefdom. Then, in 2001, the Federal Department of Education, which shouldn't exist if the states are responsible for education, passes the 'No Child Left Behind Act.' Look. I don't disagree with the concept, you know, accountability. It's just this tendency to swing the pendulum from one side to the other. What?"

"Nothing," Ed says. "I'm fascinated. I've never heard any of this."

"Ever since budgets have been slashed, state test scores all over the country are dropping. And everyone knows other countries are passing us in education. We used to think of it as an *investment,* but now it's an expense. Every year there are new challenges and rules with good intentions. They're all necessary, but they usually aren't funded.

"And don't get me started on the newest buzzword-compliance. Half the kids have some kind of things we have to manage. Medicine, allergies, or special services like an Individual Education Plan. You'll see. All of this is fine but *fund it*! Like I said, they keep adding rules and things with no additional money. So, the basics have to get cut. The budget pie is the same dollar amount or less every year, so it has to be sliced differently. And now we have to *charge* kids to play sports. A lot of the time these are the kids that can least afford it. There have been no raises for years, we can't afford new textbooks, we are way behind in technology, and it goes on and on. For some reason the government has zeroed in on teachers; pass your state tests and keep the school accredited. But no new taxes to help. Really?"

Kilo's rant is over.

Vice Principal Derry has overheard part of the conversation and doesn't like the negativity. He waits to bring it up at another time. It's an hour later and Ed and Kilo's mission is almost complete.

"Not too bad," Kilo says, admiring their work.

"Maybe half-an-hour to go. And don't worry about the germs, they're good for you. Builds up your resistance. Every germ ever made is in this building. You'll be sick as a dog this year until you become immune to just about everything. I haven't sneezed in years, so cheer up!"

Ed arrives at Anita's house on Thursday evening with chicken take-out. An hour later they move to the living room. Ed has a beer and Anita has red wine.

"How is your classroom set-up going?" Anita asks. "One more day this week, then Labor Day, and then the little ones arrive. Sure you don't want some help?"

"No, I'm fine. Thank God for Kilo. I've been telling you how much he's helped me. He's pretty funny, too. He calls me Public Ed."

"For public education. I get it. He's a character. I've told you that his name has nothing to do with the metric system, right?"

"About ten times. I figure his parents were hippies."

"He's a really good guy," Anita continues. "A bit cynical, kind of mysterious, but you'll like that. He's an excellent teacher. The kids love him."

"How old do you think he is?" Ed asks.

"I'm not sure. Mid-fifties, early-fifties?"

"He doesn't look, or act, that old."

"I agree. And he's kind of cute."

"Listen to you! A little crush?"

"Have you met Mr. White, yet?"

"Good deflection. Sure, Guy White. You know what they used to call him as a kid?"

"White guy. Even though he's black. Everyone knows that. You want to talk about the mysterious! That man is one of a kind!"

Anita goes on to tell Ed some other tid-bits she has heard. After a few minutes, Ed gets serious.

"I want to talk to you about Derry," Ed says.

"Kilo says he's a jackass. Do you know him?"

"I don't want to say too much. It wouldn't be professional of me to say that man is a paranoid, vindictive, self-centered bully."

"Way to stay professional."

"I'm biting my tongue. Just be careful. He doesn't get along with *anyone*. And, he's obsessed with being a principal, so he hunts for anything wrong in his school that would harm his reputation. He wants to be the hero. Do you know what the kids call him?"

"What?"

"Derry Queen the King of Mean."

"That's great!" Ed responds. "But why is he still around?"

"Because he gets things done. The feeling is he just needs to mature, learn some people skills, you know, slow down a little. Oh, and watch out for his sidekick, Nurse Atlas."

"Yeah, why are they always together?"

"Because they're both power-hungry. Atlas supposedly got terminated from a hospital in D.C. because she couldn't get along with anyone. The only good thing is no kid *ever* wants to go to the nurse. She's a beast. Keep an eye on both of them."

It's the Friday before school starts and everyone is scrambling. Ed has a list of things Derry wants to be done in his classroom before the students arrive. Fortunately, Kilo is ready and available to help.

"Hey," Ed says. "Remember how we were talking about the public education system, and how it's a giant bureaucratic mess? I think I have a solution."

"You have a solution to fix public education? Really? After a couple days?"

"I'm thinking we should start a new country. And open a new school."

"I like it! Wait. What? A new country? Where? How? I'm all ears."

"Start a new country. Blank piece of paper. No stupid rules."

"OK, I'm in," Kilo replies. "But where?"

"Let's pull down my wall map. Well, wait. How about that part of Michigan? Not the glove part, but isn't there a little chunk of land in the north that's on the border with Canada? Let's take a look."

Kilo points to the spot. "Yeah, right here. Up north. What do they call this thing, an isthmus or something?"

"I don't know. You're the science guy."

"You're the geography guy!" Kilo retorts.

"What about Detroit? It's not far from there. And didn't everybody leave?"

"Nah. We'd never agree on the price; how much they would pay *us* to take it. But I love this other spot. It's perfect! And I bet no one lives there now. It's probably freezing in the winter and giant mosquitoes in the summer."

"You just described the Midwest," Ed says.

"And I'm pretty sure we could buy it, or maybe storm it with a few friends. There can't be many people there. What is there to do? Who would want to live *there*?"

"Then why do we want it again?"

"Exactly. Because nobody else wants it. It's like the island of misfit toys. You know, where the reindeer wants to be a dentist. Wait. I've got it! The isthmus of misfits!"

"No," Ed replies. "Misfit Isthmus!"

"That's great! A name and a place. What else could you possibly need?"

"Not rules," Ed says.

"No rules! We get rid of all the stupid rules. Like, OK, I got one. You know that 'i' before 'e' except after 'c'? GONE! 'I' will always be first. At everything. Let's say the alphabet is going to lunch. 'I' goes first!"

"That's a good one; fine by me," says Ed.

"And movies. No movies over two hours. If you can't tell a story in two hours or less, then you're fired!"

"That sounds like a rule," Ed says.

"Oh, yeah. I've got another one. The whole metric system thing."

"Toss it?"

"No. Better. Metric *time*. Think about it," Kilo says casually.

"Huh?"

"It's supposed to be so simple. Metric weight, metric distance. Why not metric time? 100 seconds in a minute, 100 minutes in an hour, 100 hours in a day!"

"Brilliant!" Ed says. "Wait. 100 hours in a day? We need to think about that one. Maybe just weekends. Anyway, what about no acronyms? Who the hell even knows what the word means?"

"You're right. It sounds like a pimple medicine. And maybe no vowels? But we might have just put Vanna White out of business," Kilo says, enjoying the conversation.

"Whoa, slow down, cowboy. What if, and I'm just thinking. We might need vowels, but what about no word having more than two syllables? I mean, think about the time we waste. Ex-ag-er-a-ted. Five syllables!"

"Good point," Kilo replies. "And wait. How about no two people can have the same name. I *hate* that."

"First name or last name?" Ed asks.

"Both! One Tom, one Dick, one Harry, one Jones. I call Jones!"

"Fair enough. Now, what if they die? Do we retire the name, or reissue it?"

"Retire it. Like a sports jersey. There's only *one* number three on the New York Yankees" Kilo states.

"And his whole name is only two syllables! Babe Ruth."

All of a sudden, the two men look up and see Derry and Atlas leering from the doorway.

"If you *children* are finished," Derry says, "I'd like to start checking off your room preparation lists. For when the *real* children get here."

Kilo whispers to Ed, "And no checklists."

Chapter Three

The three-day Labor Day weekend flies by. Ed brings some final chores home to work on, like attendance sheets and creating a PowerPoint highlighting his background and path to teaching. Ed hopes the kids will find it interesting. He also went to an open house with Anita in an effort to find his own home. Luckily there are many available, although this particular house is a no-go.

Tuesday morning. The first day of school! Ed didn't think he'd ever hear *that* again. He remembers for a moment how his late mother always insisted on taking first-day pictures of Anita and him.

He parks and walks up to the all-brick building, thinking about his journey to become a teacher. He smiles at the satisfaction of his achievement. So far, so good. But, he knows the tough part lies ahead.

Ed inserts his key in the classroom door. He hears a familiar voice behind him. Kilo Jones greets Ed.

"Showtime," Kilo says, "Are you ready for your first day?"

"I guess. I mean, I think so."

"One thing nice down here, it's a pretty quiet hallway. We're lucky with this layout since it is away from the main corridor. You mostly just see our other sixth-grade teachers, and we all share the same students."

"Now," Kilo continues. "Remember the schedule. Two classes, lunch, two classes, and then teacher planning during the fifth block. Oh, and remind me to show you a few of the other hallways. It's always interesting."

Kilo continues his pep talk.

"OK, Public Ed. For today, don't be nervous. They're sixth graders and it's their first day in middle school. They are a little intimidated so don't be afraid to be firm. They don't figure out how to torture us for a few weeks. Now, three things to remember, in addition to the four-hundred things everyone has told you. One, they're kids. They are supposed to be annoying."

"And?" Ed asks.

"Don't forget you were a kid. Adults are supposed to be annoying."

"And? You said three things."

"Oh, good, I'm glad I said all three; sometimes I forget."

A little while later Ed and Kilo step out into the hallway and stand in front of their classroom doors to greet the excited and apprehensive students, and then enter their rooms behind the last child.

The kids in Ed's classroom scatter to find seats.

"Good morning," Ed says from the front of the room. "I'm Mr.—"

There is a light knock on the door and a student comes in. An interruption already? It is a young girl who says her name is Cecelia, a student Ed has not met yet.

"Hi," Cecelia says tentatively. "I'm a student aide. I need to take Jake Laguna to the Guidance Office." She has a pass in her hand.

"Do you have a subpoena?" Ed asks for fun.

"No. I'm a girl!"

There are only a few giggles. *Rough crowd*, Ed thinks. Jake follows Cecelia out the door.

"Good morning again," Ed continues from the script he sketched out and memorized over the weekend for each of his four classes. "Just a quick note. I let you sit where you wanted because now I know where you *shouldn't* sit. You're probably all next to your friends which is fine, but if it becomes a problem, I will move you. And you two in the back, come up front to these empty seats." The two boys moan as they move.

"I'm Mr. Knudknickovich. It might be easier if I spell it."

Ed prints his name with chalk in large letters while annunciating each one.

"K-N-U-D-K-N-I-C-K-O-V-I-C-H"

Two boys, best friends and sitting next to each other, are whispering. Jamal Fowler, a thin, twelve-year-old African American boy, is leaning over and speaking softly to another student. For years now, everyone calls him 'Fowler' because there is another Jamal.

"Is he writing his name in Russian?" Fowler asks his friend in a low voice.

Andre Martinez, thirteen, Hispanic and normally loud, is leaning in to hear his friend.

"What's Russian?"

Fowler replies, "Russia. It was a giant country. You know, Cold War."

"Cold War? Is that PlayStation or XBOX?"

"Ugh, never mind."

"Well," Andre whispers, "he's going to need a bigger piece of chalk."

Logan, twelve, a pretty, blonde girl and unlikely member of this trio of best friends, schusses them.

Ed has finished writing his name and is staring at the two boys, trying out his 'stink-eye' for the first time. The room gets very quiet.

Ed underlines his name in chalk. Blake Wily, a confident, bold, and sometimes annoying twelve-year-old girl has her hand up and waits over-anxiously to be called on. She's squirming in her seat to be noticed.

Ed asks, "Do you have a question? Already?"

"How do you pronounce *that*," Blake asks in a way only kids can demonstrate disdain.

"I'm getting to that. I'm Mr.—"

Blake's hand goes up again.

"Do you have another question?"

"That's pretty long. Can we call you Mr. K?"

"My name is Mr. Knudknickovich."

"So, you don't pronounce the K? Just the first one, or *all* of them?"

"Yes," Ed replies to Blake. "You don't pronounce the K. I mean no, you don't pronounce the K. Technically, since you don't pronounce the K, then calling me Mr. K wouldn't make sense. It's a silent K."

Blake asks, "Can we call you Mr. Silent K?"

"Um, well, sure. Yes, you can call me Mr. Silent K."

Andre jumps into the conversation.

"I don't get it. A silent letter means it doesn't sound like nothing. Can we call you Mr. Nothing?" Fowler is rolling his eyes. The other kids are watching closely.

Ed replies, "Not going to happen, Mister. OK, my turn to mispronounce *your* names. I have the attendance sheet. Moving on. Time for the name game. I had a professor do this and I always wanted to try it."

Ed Knudknickovich, now Mr. Silent K, asks a girl in the first row her name, repeats it, and continues the pattern, adding one and saying all of the other names back in the same order each time. He keeps messing up a boy's name in the middle of the room.

"Johnny?"

"Nope."

"Jimmy?"

"Nope."

"Jackie?"

"That's a *girl's* name!"

"Wally?"

"Nope. Wait. What?"

"Arnold?"

Other kids are starting to laugh.

"No. It starts with an R."

"Ronald, Ritchie, Rickey, Robby, Rudolph—"

"It's *Randall.*"

"No, that's not it. Kidding."

Ed smiles and repeats back all twenty-seven names, including Randall. A hand goes up.

"Yes, Blake. Do you have another question?"

"You keep calling him Bob. That guy. That's not his name."

"What? Who?"

"Him, in the front row."

Ed approaches him.

"Is this true?" he asks the boy. "Your name is not Bob?"

"Yes. My name is not Bob."

"Oh! Nice to meet you, Not-Bob! Now, a little about myself. When I'm not working, I like to fish for fish, bark for bark, fly a fly, and duck a duck."

A hand goes up.

"Yes, Blake?"

"Are you *sure* you're a teacher?"

The morning flies by and it's lunchtime. Ed sits down at his desk, exhausted. Kilo stops at Ed's door.

Kilo asks Ed, "You aren't going to eat in the quote 'teacher's lounge?' It's decorated in early reform-school furniture."

"I've seen it. I think I'm just going to sit and relax for a few minutes. How long do we get again?"

"Twenty-five minutes, the fastest part of the day. And then just two classes to go before planning. Are you sure you don't want to come with me? You hear the best stories!"

"I'll try it tomorrow. I have to decompress. Man, that was nuts! My last class had twenty-eight students all talking at the same time."

"And the day's not over. See you soon."

Kilo leaves while Ed eats. He looks at the back of his potato chip bag. He stops and reads the trivia portion of the bag that says a person can't lick their own elbow, so he tries it. Ed does not see the two people watching from his door as he twists his arm and neck awkwardly. No luck; can't lick it. Vice Principal Derry and Nurse Rhoda Atlas, a large woman in a white smock, step away unseen.

Nurse Atlas says to Derry as they walk, "You better keep your eye on that one."

"That's what I've been saying. We shouldn't hire teachers who aren't teachers."

"Oh, right, *he's* the career transitionary. The comedian. Anita Gold's brother."

"Yes. He's the joke writer from New York City. The *real* joke is that we hired him. I voted 'no' in the interview, but I lost because he charmed everyone else. And yes, his sister probably helped him every step of the way."

"It's pretty obvious you don't like him. How come?"

"Well," Derry continues, "the other beef I have is student test scores. This pretend-teacher can really mess up my numbers if his students bomb the state's tests. That goes on *my* record. Plus, I did some checking. Half of all transitionary teachers quit after a year, and most are gone by five years. It just seems like we are wasting our time. I think we could have hired a better teacher with more experience."

"So now what?"

"Well, I'm usually right, so we get him. I might need your help, but we'll get him. Don't forget he's on probation the first year. He can be let go for just about anything, or not be invited back next year."

Later in the day, during planning, Kilo takes Ed for a walk.

"Come on," Kilo says. "I want to show you a couple of places in the school you probably haven't seen yet. And it's fun to walk around the halls and just listen. Most teachers keep their doors open and what you hear can be free entertainment. Even during the first day, seventh and eighth grade do a lot of reviewing."

Ed and Kilo walk slowly down a hall. They are going door to door, listening from out of sight.

"The eighth-grade hall is the best. This is Ms. Walker's class. She's a beast."

The two hear Ms. Walker's frustrated voice.

"Nazi! Nazi! Nazi! How many times do I have to say it?"

A surprised Ed says, "What is she railing about?"

They hear Ms. Walker again.

"The answer is *not* C! It's B."

Ed and Kilo giggle and keep walking.

Kilo says, "Here's Mr. Balzac's room. And yes, it's his real name. He's related to some famous writer or author or movie star or something. Let's see what he's yelling about."

"That's it, Dwayne," Balzac says. "I told you the next time you argue I call home. What's your mom's cell number?"

"I don't know her cell number," Dwayne replies. "I haven't visited her in jail yet."

"Oh, boy," Kilo says. "Let's keep going. This is Ms. Camper's English class. Listen."

"Great job, Tory. That's a metaphor."

"Come on, Ms. C," Tory says. "That's at least a meta-five!"

The two pass Kwaji who is speaking to a student in the hallway, and Ed and Kilo slow down to listen.

"Jimmy," Kwaji says. "Where are you going?"

"I got sent to the office."

"Why?"

"Well, I kind of punched a kid in an inappropriate place."

"Inappropriate place? You mean like in the library?"

"No," Jimmy replies. "Down *there*." His eyes point to his waste.

"Oh, no! Let me go with you."

Ed and Kilo keep walking. They hear yelling from another teacher.

"Why does everybody down here sound so angry?" Ed asks innocently.

"Fourteen-year olds. Listen. Ms. Ewe is a screamer."

"Nein! Nein! Nein!"

"She teaches German?" Ed asks.

"Math," Kilo says.

"Then why is she yelling—"

"The square root of eighty-one is nine!"

"Oh," Ed replies.

"One more," Kilo says. "Mrs. Clanton always has some strange kids."

"OK," they hear her say to her class. "Brandon, what is the largest star in our solar system?"

"Um, the Kardashians?"

"Told ya," Kilo says.

The first day of school is over. Anita gets home late from her arduous role as a high school principal. They share stories.

"They call you Mr. Silent K? How cute," Anita says.

"Did I tell you how hard this job is?" Ed asks.

"I'm pretty sure I know," Anita says, yawning. "One-hundred-seventy-nine days to go."

Ed turns in as he prepares for the next, long, day.

Chapter Four

The week flies by. Ed and Kilo talk after school.

"Let me share some more mentoring wisdom," Kilo says. "A couple of things you are definitely going to need to know as a rookie. *Never* yell. It just escalates things and is entertaining to the students. Don't give warnings. Either discipline or don't. And don't be afraid to call parents. It is usually very helpful. If you can get them. And—"

"Wait," Ed says. "I got this. A fifty-five-gallon drum of hand sanitizer."

"No! Who have you been talking to? Do *not* let these other teachers influence you! I am your sensei."

"Gee, OK, OK. I thought it was just common sense...ay."

"Good one. Now, remember I told you to *embrace* the germs. The faster the better. You'll get sick a couple times, especially the first few weeks. You probably won't die. Anyway, most teachers die from boredom. Kidding. But you want every germ you can get. Rub your eyes every hour. Make sure you never buy antibacterial soap for home. Lick and roll around on the thirty-year-old carpet in the library. Oh, and always put your hands in the trash can before leaving for the day. Kids spit in there, throw snotty tissues in there. It's a cornucopia of viruses."

"I think I'm going to throw up," Ed says.

"Good! That means it's already working!"

"So, remember. Don't let the old-time teachers ruin you. And don't be afraid to hold your students accountable for their behavior. There's no quicker way for Derry to get you than to have poor classroom management. If you get a kid being very disruptive, send him to me and I'll keep them in my room. Miss Vega has already done it this week. We call it the Prisoner Exchange Program. I know I grumble a lot, but I also want to see people succeed. I don't mind helping out, so use me."

Since it is Friday, Ed decides to eat with the other teachers. The teacher's lounge is busy with activity; conversations overlap and merge. Bells from microwaves ding. This is supposed to be a place for teachers to relax, but it seems very hectic to Ed. *At least it should be a good place to bond,* Ed thinks to himself, *since all the sixth-grade teachers have lunch at the same time.*

Miss Vega, the young but feisty math teacher, addresses the room.

"Did anyone get a chance to read the email that Guidance is starting an exercise class?"

"Exercise," Ed says. "I thought it said *exorcism.* I've already sent three kids!"

Mr. Larkin says, "Well, I had my driver's license out on my desk and Blake asked if she could look at it. Then she says, 'You're an organ donor? Who would want them?' I just bit my tongue. Wait, and then she says, 'Is this expiration date for you?'"

"Oh," Miss Vega says. "I heard we are all getting student aides."

"Does the C.D.C. know about this?" Kilo asks. "I was looking at a few of my textbooks yesterday and you know the large stamp on the inside cover with two columns? One says, 'student name' and the other lists the condition of the book? Some kid from last year wrote in 'Shelly Brown,' and under condition wrote, 'dumb blonde.'"

"I'm having a fun day," says Ms. Rivalry, one of the librarians who usually eats with the sixth-grade teachers.

"I was in the office part of the library, you know, behind the glass. And you know that row of computers facing the office? Well, I just happen to notice Jake Laguna typing in 'STDs,' and by the time I got out there he had pressed 'images!'"

"It wasn't restricted?"

"No. And it was disgusting!"

It's hard to tell who is talking to who and about what. Guy White, the middle-aged, quirky English teacher is writing on a piece of yellow legal paper.

Kilo asks, "Guy, what are you working on now? What's your newest business plan?"

For some reason foreign to Ed it seems everyone wants to hear this.

"Hi, Kilo."

The roar in the room becomes quiet. All eyes are on Guy, the hapless inventor who is always willing to share his ideas.

"Well, it's been a slow month. '24-Hour Glue' went nowhere. People don't like things falling apart the next day for some reason. But tape that doesn't stick sells like crazy.

I missed out on that one because, well, isn't it the *point* of tape to stick? Anyway, I'm still hoping 'Home Alone Baby Litter' catches on, for people without daycare.

"Now my newest project, this is a winner! It's a bottled drink, clear, almost like water. It probably *will* be water. It's aimed at middle school kids, like ours, eleven to fourteen-year-olds."

"Is that it?" Kilo asks. "Another bottled water?"

"What? Oh, no. It's clear when you drink it, but it turns your pee blue."

"Did you say it turns your pee blue?" Kwaji asks, suddenly interested.

"Yes. It turns your pee blue. There's a chemical, safe of course, that makes urine come out bright blue. So, picture in your mind a twelve-year-old boy peeing."

"Are we allowed to do that?" Kilo asks.

"You know what I mean. How cool would it be if your pee was blue! Wouldn't you want to show your friends?"

"I'm not sure *that* is legal, either," Kilo says.

"You know what I mean. I even have a name for it. *Blue Stream.* I'm working on slogans for marketing. I might try *Blue Stream: Your #1 Choice.* Get it? Number one?"

Dead silence.

"Sounds like a winner," Kilo says.

"And," Guy says.

"There's more?" Miss Vega asks.

Guy continues. "I'm thinking about economies of scale. As long as I'm making a drink, I'm going to make a second one. Double my chances. If one fails, maybe the other one will fly."

"Just remember, Guy," says Miss Vega, hearing some of Guy's ideas for the first time.

"Two times zero is zero."

"Good one. Here it is. Who remembers the name of the first man in space? Hint. He was a cosmonaut."

Kilo answers first. "Illya, um, Illya Kuriakin or something? Is that it?"

"That's the guy from *Man from U.N.C.L.E.*," Ed says. "Now he's Ducky on *NCIS*."

"That's the same guy?" Kilo asks. "I didn't know that. Sounds Russian to me."

Guy stands up and goes to the chalkboard in the teacher's lounge used to write notes or announcements on.

Guy spells and says, "Y-U-R-I. Yuri Gagarin."

"That's it!" Ms. Rivalry says. "Shouldn't you science and history guys know that?"

"I know Sputnik," Ed says. "And the dog they sent up."

"They sent a *dog* into space?" Miss Vega asks, showing her youth. "How did they get it back?"

"Well, I'm pretty sure he's still up there. Or it was eventually pulled in by gravity and burned up."

"That's disgusting!" Veronica Vega replies.

"That's science," Kilo says.

"And so is this," Guy says.

"Now, in the United States, we have TANG. It's always associated with astronauts. It's still around, believe it or not."

Kwaji says, "I love TANG. That's the closest thing to orange juice we ever got on the island."

"Yes," Guy continues. "Powder. Orange. Stir it into water. It's iconic. But it's the USA. So, to honor the cosmonauts, now that the Cold War is over, I'm making something similar, but yellow."

Chalk in hand, Guy writes Y-U-R-I-N-E on the board.

"It's pronounced Yurine, like urine. It's bright yellow. Get it? Yuri?"

Dead silence, then everyone goes back to what they were doing.

"Sounds like a winner, Guy," Kilo says and pats him on the back.

Lunchtime is just about over. Kwaji erases the chalkboard as the teachers gather their stuff to go and walk their students back from the cafeteria.

Ed and Kilo walk together.

"That Guy is pretty unique," Ed says.

Later that day the first week of classes is over.

"How was your first week?" Anita asks Ed when she gets home.

"You know, it was hectic, but in a good way. I'm beat, though. It zapped my energy. How about you?"

"Oh, the usual. No surprises. Hey, are you looking at houses again this weekend?"

"Trying to get rid of me, Sis? Kidding. My agent and I are supposed to look at a few on Sunday. If I'm awake by then."

"That tired, huh?"

"The standing, the walking, the paperwork. It's all draining. Who knew teaching was so hard? I mean except for you."

"People think it's easy. Summers off, short days. They have no idea how much work it is, or how much work we bring home."

"I never knew," confirms Ed. "Even so, I'm glad I made this decision. I can see how it can be rewarding. And yeah, there are a couple of problem kids, but overall I feel good about everything. I'm glad you talked me into this, at least so far, anyway."

"So how many kids do you have?"

"Well, four classes, say twenty-eight per class."

"That's not too bad. Wait until you have ninety tests or papers to grade."

"Yeah, I already thought of that."

"Good," Anita says. "Now get some rest. You'll need it."

Chapter Five

The students start their weekend as well. Best friends Andre Martinez and Jamal Fowler head to the house of their mutual friend and classmate, Logan Click, who meets them at the front door. It is Saturday around noon, the normal rousing time for pre-teens.

"No one's home?" Andre asks.

"No," a sleepy Logan replies. The medication she takes for depression because of her father's death keeps her a tad groggy.

The boys come inside. The three have been in the same classes for five years, ever since Fowler moved to Farmwood. Logan, always fairly quiet, made the unusual choice of friends after her father died.

"Where's the booze?" Andre asks. As the leader of the pack, the other two are used to his shenanigans.

"*That's* why you came over?"

"That's not why *I* came over," Fowler says, hiding a secret crush on Logan.

Jamal Fowler looks younger than his age. Is it the glasses? The short hair? The skinny frame? Fowler is a typical follower, his role in the unlikely trio.

"'That's not why I came over,'" Andre says, mimicking Fowler.

"So?" Fowler exclaims. "And be quiet."

"The booze," Logan says. "I don't think my mother even drinks."

"All women drink," states Andre. "Don't you watch *Real Housewives?*"

"Watch what?" Logan and Fowler say at the same time.

"Anyway," Andre continues. "The booze. It's usually hidden. They don't want anyone to know they drink all day."

He is rummaging through the kitchen cabinets. "Whoa!"

"You find it?" Fowler asks.

"Look at all this microwave popcorn," Andre says. "That's for later. Keep looking."

Fowler says, "Hey, Logan. Why is your silverware in this drawer? It should be in *this* drawer, near the sink. See, the fridge is here, then the sink. So, as you go by you can grab a fork or spoon. Why is it all the way on the other side of the kitchen?"

"Forget that, *iCarly*. We got work to do," Andre continues. "Where's the booze? Who cares where the spoons are? Wait, got it! Cream-duh-minty. What is this stuff?"

"It's liqueur."

"I know it's liquor, Fowler. Gee, you could at least say it right."

"No," Fowler says. "It's pronoun—"

"Oh, this smells like crap," Andre cuts him off. "And it looks green! I think its French mouthwash or something. And it tastes like crap. I think it's Leprechaun pee!"

"Let me see it," Fowler says.

"Wait," says Andre. "You're going to drink booze?"

"I might."

"Well, you ain't drinking mine. Give me that back. Let's see here. Eighteen percent alcohol. Eighteen percent out of what?"

"One hundred," Fowler responds.

"Never mind, you."

"I don't know about this," Fowler says haltingly. "I've never seen anyone drinking a green drink at one of my parent's parties."

"That because you were probably reading a book, instead of finishing beer bottles like me."

"Still. It looks more like an elixir to me."

"A what? You don't lick it, you drink it! I'm having more," Andre says.

Logan comes into the kitchen.

"Hey, Andre. Why do you have a green mustache? You found it?"

"Yeah, while you were upstairs."

"Well, you have to replace what you drink."

"I know *that*. That's for when we're done. What we have to do now, see, is mix it. They're always mixing stuff to make drinks," Andre says, obviously a pro. "Fancy drinks, I think they're called."

Logan asks, "Mix it with what?"

"Soda? I guess."

"We don't have any. My mom usually doesn't buy any."

"Where is your mom?" Jamal asks.

"Giving guitar lessons at the center."

"At the center of what?" Andre inquires.

"The Senior Center."

"So, when I'm a senior I have to play guitar? Should we be practicing now?"

"Not a *high school* senior," Fowler retorts. "An old person. Although, you might be that old in high school."

"Why I oughta…"

"Where's your brother?" Fowler asks Logan.

"He goes, too. Mom says the old people love him. Alex says he likes the wrinkly people."

Fowler responds, "Why do old people—"

Andre cuts him off. "Milk! We can use milk!"

"We don't have any of that, either."

"Who runs out of milk and soda? Let me see. What's this? Heavy cream. The date's still good."

Andre creates a concoction that looks like a thick, emerald milkshake. Logan is on the couch, watching TV.

"Can we look around?" Fowler asks Logan.

"Sure, but I'm tired," Logan replies. "Just don't break anything."

Fowler follows Andre down the hallway and into a bedroom, which turns out to be Mrs. Click's.

"What are we doing?" Fowler asks.

"We're looking around. Who knows? Maybe underwear."

"Underwear? Eew!"

"Who knows. Let's just look for stuff."

"I don't know…"

"Just come on!"

"But Logan's mom might come home," Fowler reminds Andre.

"I know *that*. It doesn't matter. We'll hear her and run. Now help me look around."

"Are you sure?"

"Logan said we could. Now, wait! Come here quick!" Andre says.

Andre is holding a bra in one hand and the elixir in the other. His green mustache is still present and disturbing looking.

"Look!" Andre says.

"Oh, my God."

"Here. Take it. See what size it is."

"I'm not touching it!" Fowler exclaims.

"Just take it. There's probably a tag somewhere. Haven't you seen your mother's?"

"Eew!"

"What? You never checked out your mother's underwear drawer?"

"Yes. Wait, no. Just give it to me. Three four C."

"It's 34C, you dope."

"Why's it got two sizes?" Fowler innocently asks. "Cause there are two boobs?"

"What?"

"It's got letters *and* numbers. How come?"

"Because one is the size, like your pants. And the letter, well, that's the hotness scale. C is pretty good, but D is better."

"How come in school C is *better* than a D?"

"That's it. Give me that back," Andre demands. "You don't get to touch it no more! You don't even know the hotness scale! Look at this thing. These are shoulder boulders. Hey, go check on Logan."

Fowler leaves as Andre keeps snooping.

Fowler is back and says, "She's sleeping."

"You scared the crap out of me! Come here. You got to see this." Andre is leaning over a shoebox.

"Polaroids!" Fowler says excitedly.

"No, you dope. They're pictures."

"Before digital, there were—"

"Would you be quiet! Now, let's see. That's Logan's mother! And she's wearing a bathing suit!"

"That's a string bikini," Fowler says.

"I don't care what it's made of. She's hot. I'm taking these!"

"Whoa. Wow! Wait. What do you mean?"

"I'm taking some. Here. You can have one."

"Take them?" Fowler asks. "Take them where? We can't take them! She'll know we took them! Where did you get that box from?"

"Under the bed. What if we take them…and…we get copies made and then bring them back?"

"Copy them *where*?" a reluctant Fowler asks.

"Don't you have a copy machine? Now give me these."

"You can't take them!"

"We'll bring them back!"

"When are we ever going to be in Logan's mom's bedroom again? That's stealing. We're going to get in *so* much trouble."

Andre replies, "I'm not leaving—"

"Wait. I got it! Take pictures of them with your phone. Then we *got to* put them back," a flustered Fowler says.

"Alright, alright. I will, I will. Crap! My grandma took my phone for a week. Use yours!"

"I don't know," Fowler says.

"Just give me your phone! And you better send them to me or I'll beat the crap out of you!"

Fowler reluctantly hands over his smartphone.

The two amateur sleuths take some pictures of the pictures. It's Fowler's idea to try not to include the woman's face. The quality is terrible, but they don't care. Fowler wants to delete them as soon as possible but can't stand the thought of losing the pictures for good.

"I promise I will send them to you. Now let's *please* get out of here!"

"Wait," Andre says. "I think I'm going to puke. I don't feel so good. I think this *is* mouthwash. Oh…"

"We're leaving," Fowler demands.

The two boys leave Logan on the couch and head out the front door. A confused neighbor will find a puddle of green throw-up on the sidewalk later that day.

Chapter Six

Another day of classes ends, and Ed walks into Kilo's classroom during their planning block. He is carrying a large binder and assorted papers. Ed is getting the feeling that Derry is waiting for him to slip up and wants to cover all his bases.

"Hey, Kilo. Can I ask you some more questions about the lesson plan thing?"

"That's right! Newbies have to do *daily* lesson plans."

"And hand them in," Ed replies. "Don't you?"

"Well, because I teach the same subject every year, I don't do them. Or I use an old one and change the date. I mean, I'm probably *supposed* to do them, but…"

"Oh," Ed says. "So, no one checks them?"

"No one checks *mine.* Almost everyone else has to do them, and for sixth-grade, Derry checks them. I've heard he's pretty demanding."

"Great. Any suggestions?"

"Well, do you have the lesson plan form? Let's knock some out."

The two men work side by side for an hour or so, right up to the bell. They use the history curriculum book and the

Virginia Department of Education resources to complete a week's worth of plans.

"Done," Kilo says. "They're beautiful!"

"Now what?" Ed asks.

"Just keep writing the perfect lesson plan on paper, follow all the stuff in the binders from the department of Ed, and all the stuff from the school board office, and all the stuff from the history chair."

"And then what?"

"Then do whatever you want or need to do to keep the kids' attention. That's the key."

"But doesn't Derry pop into classrooms? What if I'm not following the plan?"

"It could happen. But if the kids are engaged, then that's the most important thing. To me, anyway. You can just say you are ahead or behind. Listen, your job is to *teach*, not to recite or regurgitate. Kids first, boss second. That's my rule. But with Derry, be very afraid..."

Once again, Derry hears the men talking, and is determined to catch Ed not following a lesson plan.

A week later Ed is at his door greeting his students as they arrive. Ed has some new, but unconventional, ideas for this class to keep the students engaged, and follows the last child into the classroom.

"OK," Ed starts. "We have a lot to do today. Who can tell me, oh, Mr. Derry."

Derry has slithered into the room and takes a seat in the back. He has his trusty laptop that he keeps his notes on when he observes teachers.

"Just ignore me," Derry says. "I'm not here. But please hand me your lesson plan."

"Of course," Ed says, handing over the paper while trying not to appear nervous. His palms are moist and his mouth is dry as the lesson plan does not match what he has planned for today. *Just my luck*, Ed is thinking. *And this is my toughest class because of rowdy behavior. Of course.*

"OK," Ed starts. "Who can tell me what I wrote on the board means. Manifest Destiny."

Jake Laguna, ever the wise guy, speaks out and says, "Wasn't Beyoncé with them?"

"Jake, we've talked about this. First, raise your hand. Second, no irrelevant comments."

Ed can feel his face getting flush.

"So?" Ed asks again. "Any takers? Well, then who is my Google-er today?"

Logan raises her hand and walks to the front. She types into the computer that shows up on the large screen on the front wall.

"Your what?" Derry asks.

"I designate a student to use the computer each day. Sometimes we get stuck on a date, or a word, or a spelling. There is a calendar by my desk. It's Logan's turn today."

Derry is typing furiously on his laptop. Ed is smart enough to realize this is probably not a good thing.

Logan has found a definition of Manifest Destiny and it shines on the screen. Ed then has Logan pull up visuals like the period-painting *Niagara* by Albert Bierstadt.

"OK," Ed continues. "I want everyone to write down in your journal the definition of Manifest Destiny. I'll give you a couple of minutes."

Ed walks around the room slowly, then asks for a volunteer to give the definition and the resulting issues.

Fowler's is one of a couple of hands raised in the air. Ed calls on him.

"Indians," Fowler says.

"Good. But what was the problem?"

"Well, it was their land. And they had already been pushed out all over the place."

Derry is watching both Ed and the kids closely.

"Excellent," Ed says. "We know that as people were moving west, they ran into something called the 'Indian Problem,' like Fowler said. After the Civil War, the army was put in charge of protecting people moving west. This caused some conflicts." Ed calls on Amy who has her hand up.

"We learned last year that ever since people came to America, they pushed the Indians further out. The people from Europe had better weapons and more and more people just kept coming."

"True," Ed says, impressed by the statement. "And we are going to talk more about the Indian Wars in the 1800s. And we are going to tie it into Tolerance Week that is going on here at school. It's about accepting and living with people different than you. Americans went onto Indian land and said, 'Get out,' or, 'if you want to stay you have to be more like us and be farmers and have jobs.'"

"We were bullies," Blake says.

"In a way, yes. But you have to remember the context, or the times. Different times, different ideas. And when people started saying 'Manifest Destiny,' that means they will stop at nothing to go west, that it was America's destiny to go from ocean to ocean. You could say it was an excuse and showed how we thought we were superior to the Native

American People and didn't see anything wrong with what they were doing. They felt the continent was so large the Indians could easily find new places to live."

"My way or the highway," Jake says.

"Good point, Jake."

Ed goes over to his laptop.

"I'm going to show you a video clip from a cartoon called *Go Go Gophers.*"

"From *Adult Swim?*" Jake cracks, and promptly gets the stink-eye from Ed.

"No. It's old. Very old. Older than me. But it shows every stereotype. You'll see Indians portrayed as weak, lazy, and not very bright. They talk funny and look strange. It was very disrespectful. Now, the gophers—"

"What's a gopher?" Amy asks.

"Oh. Hold on. I'll show you. Here's a picture on the screen."

"They're so cute," Logan says. "Where can I get one?"

"Alright," Ed says. "On the cartoon, the gophers were the army guys; they were in charge. The main gopher in charge, as a matter of fact, looks and acts like Teddy Roosevelt. The president. But that's another story."

"I thought Trump is the president?" Amy asks.

"That's why it's another story. Now, the Indians in the cartoon were always in the way, bumbling around. It was out west; in the time period we are studying."

"You had to watch cartoons about *history* when you were a kid?" Jake asks.

"Look, it was *way* before *Sponge Bath Bob Pants.* Just watch."

"Haha," Logan says. "You said it wrong."

"Just watch. Quietly."

About ten minutes of the cartoon plays on the screen. The kids are fascinated, even with the crude drawings and silly story. It leads to a productive talk about tolerance, diversity, and stereotyping.

"OK," Ed says. "Pack up. Almost bell time! Let's get ready to go. Nice job today."

The room begins to empty out as the bell rings. Ed feels good about the lesson and expects kudos from Derry, who stays behind in the room.

"What the hell was *that*," Derry says unexpectedly. "I don't even know where to start! Google-er? YouTube? *Cartoons?* Not to mention none of this is on your lesson plan."

Derry steps closer to Ed, an intimidation tactic.

Ed counters. "Wait a second. I used approved methods. I split the topics into chunks, I used technology for the visual learners."

"You broke every rule we have," an angry Derry states. "You can't tell about how we *used* to talk about the Indians! You can't teach about the past!"

"What? This is a *history* class!" Ed exclaims, getting angrier.

"You know what I mean. You don't tell them how it has been rewritten. Not at this age. It just confuses them."

Students for the next class start to tentatively walk in. Derry's presence sends them scrambling.

"Wait in the hall!" Derry says. The kids leave.

"But the comparison gets them involved," Ed replies. "It got their attention! I tied it into tolerance week. I showed them right and wrong, how opinions evolve over time."

"We don't *show* the wrong. We don't *test* on the wrong. Do you know how many calls I'll get from angry parents that first of all, why is my kid watching cartoons in school, and second, why were they watching a cross-eyed Indian? Jesus, I don't know what to do with you!"

"Listen, I'm not some twenty-two-year-old. This is not professional. You're right in my face. And, the kids *got* it!"

"You listen to *me,*" Derry counters. "First, forty percent of yours and mine evaluation is based on test scores. What you did just now is sabotage. I don't think gophers are on the state test! I'm certainly not going to let you ruin my stats. Second, this was not an approved lesson plan. This is why we shouldn't hire people who aren't teachers."

Derry's walkie-talkie radio comes on and he is called to the office. He wasn't done with Ed.

"As of right now, this minute, you are on probation. You are on improve or remove." He was talking through clenched teeth.

"And if I get *one* phone call, just one about cartoons, you are *gone.*"

Ed is flustered and frustrated, as well as bewildered.

Test scores? Lesson plans? Covering your butt? This is public education, Ed is thinking*?*

Ed rants to Anita when she gets home, late as usual. None of this was news to her, but she understands her brother's view.

"You can't be put on improve or remove after a few weeks," she says. "He's just blustering, making a power play. Tell me again what you did."

Ed explains the Google-er, the gophers, the whole nine yards. It didn't help when Anita laughed about the gophers.

"Look," she says, feeling stuck in the middle. "I can call Principal Cutty if you'd like."

"No. I have a feeling somehow that would make it worse. I'm out looking for a house to buy, so this has to work. I have to figure this out. I guess I have to *conform*. No wonder teachers are stressed. And this emphasis on state test scores, give me a break. That's one day out of one-hundred-and-eighty."

"You won't hear me disagree, Ed, but this is the new reality. You can't fight this one."

"Well, I wish I could just teach."

"Spoken like a true teacher. But those days are over. I can look at your lesson plans if you want."

"No. You don't get home before 8:00. You have your own priorities. I'll work with Kilo some more, even though he laughed when I told him what happened, and he made a cross-eyed face at me."

"Just let me know how I can help. You'll have days like this. Don't get discouraged."

"Oh, I won't. I'm not going to let this guy win. But I don't mind telling you I'm feeling stressed, or anxious. Between Derry and looking for a house I'm getting a little overwhelmed."

"How is house-hunting going?" Anita asks. "I wish I could help more."

"I've narrowed it down to two or three. I got to tell you, I can't believe how *cheap,* or inexpensive, houses are here! I looked at what my mortgage payment would probably be and it's half what I paid a month for rent in the city."

"Believe me, I know."

"But I have to say, if I relied solely on my teacher salary, I don't know how they do it. Some of the new teachers can't even afford cable."

"Well, trust me, I know. It's almost embarrassing when I hire teachers. And most of them have student loans of forty or fifty-thousand dollars. That's why a lot of them have to room together."

"I never thought about it until I got here. And my teacher's check is spread out over twelve months so it's even smaller. Boy, am I glad I have some money saved."

"Once you get a house and things calm down at school, you'll feel better."

"I know. And I'll be able to give you a bedroom and your garage back when I finally move my stuff out. And in a weird way, I'll feel more like part of the community by having a house here."

"Hang in there. Thanksgiving break is within sight. Every day you are in school you'll get more confidence."

"Thanks, Sis."

Chapter Seven

Kilo did indeed help Ed and the next few weeks went more smoothly. At home, Ed made an offer on a house after looking at it a second time with Anita. It is a 3/2 ranch and only a few blocks from her. Things in Ed's world are starting to settle down.

Ed and Kilo arrive early as usual on this Wednesday morning. It is the first 'Lunch-Pals Day.'

"So, Kilo, what is it we are supposed to do today?" Ed asks.

"Teach."

"No, I mean at lunch?"

"Eat."

"I guess you didn't read the email," Ed concluded.

"If I did, I ignored it."

"It didn't happen yet."

"Then how would I have read it?"

"No, the *email* came out, but the *event* didn't happen yet. Some 'Lunch-Box Day.'"

"Must be new. Never heard of it."

"Here, let me pull it up and put it on the Smart Board screen. It's from Cutty. 'In order to continue our goal of building relationships with our students, I am asking all teachers to eat in the cafeteria this Wednesday. Based on your input, this event, 'Lunch-Pals Day' will occur on the first Wednesday of each month. Please mark this on your calendar. Let's make every effort to interact with as many students as possible. Thank you for your support, Principal Cutty.'"

"So, it's today?" Kilo asks.

"Yes. What do you think about it?"

"Well, I'll have to chew on it."

"Good one!"

The ruckus from the cafeteria can be heard daily in almost all parts of the school. 'Lunch-Pals Day' is no exception. Ed is sitting near the middle of a long table filled with his sixth graders.

Ed watches and then asks, "Why is nobody eating?"

"Would you eat that?" Andre asks.

"Depends. What is it?"

Andre laughs loudly. "He can't even tell what it is!"

"That's why I get pizza," Fowler says.

"Every day?" Ed asks.

"Yup."

"They have it *every* day?"

"Yup."

"What about breakfast?" Ed asks. "Do you eat that at school?"

"Yup."

"What do you have?"

"Pizza."

"What?"

"They call it 'Breakfast Pizza.' It's cut into squares instead of triangles, but I'm pretty sure it's the same thing."

"Good marketing."

"Huh?"

"Nothing," Ed replies. "Can I see your milk carton? Mm, do you always get chocolate milk?"

"We all do. The regular milk is *disgusting*!"

"This says there is twenty-eight grams of sugar in this little thing."

"Is that good?" Fowler asks.

"That's three times the sugar you should have all day! What do you drink at breakfast?"

"Chocolate milk. I told you, the other stuff is disgusting."

Logan chimes in. "My mother says they got rid of the strawberry milk because it had too much sugar in it."

"More than chocolate milk?"

"I guess so."

"And what are you eating, Logan?"

"Nuggets. I don't like the pizza."

"Are they any good?" Ed asks.

"Not really. They're usually cold. But if you put enough sauce on them, they aren't too bad."

"What kind of sauce?"

"This orange stuff. Sweet and sour, I think?"

"More sugar," Ed says. "Great. OK, wait. I've seen the menu. They have something different every day. It says stuff like 'roast beef, mashed potatoes and gravy, fresh spring vegetables.'"

"Nobody eats that stuff," Jake chimes in. "I only eat the pizza, too."

"OK," Ed says to Jake. "And what do you eat for dinner?"

"Dinner?"

"Yeah. Dinner, supper, whatever you call it."

"You mean at night?"

"Uh, yeah."

"Hot Pockets," Jake says.

"What?"

"Hot Pockets. It's like folded pizza—"

"I know what it is," Ed responds. "Is that it?"

"Well, my mom works until midnight. But sometimes we get to go to Taco Bell on Saturday."

"What about your dad?"

"What about him?"

"When does he work?"

"I don't know. I haven't seen him since second grade. Mom says he went away. Andre says that means prison, but I don't know."

Ed quickly changes the subject. "Let me ask you," Ed continues, "if you didn't eat breakfast and lunch at school, what would you do?"

"Starve."

"Oh. Well, you guys eat a lot of sugar," Ed says, going back to the original conversation.

"No wonder you all are crazy after lunch!"

"Huh?" Jake asks. "Are you going to eat?" Mr. Silent K.

"No, I'm full. I had moose eggs for breakfast. Hey, what do they do with these trays?" Ed asks.

"What do you mean?" Not-Bob says. "We throw them in the garbage."

"I wonder why we don't recycle them. They're cardboard. Blake, what are you reading? Don't tell me. It's about a werewolf who kills a vampire at the hungry games while diverging?"

"No. It's about Venus."

"Is she a new Marvel super-hero?"

"No. *She* is a planet. Earth's twin. Space?"

"Oh yeah, I've heard of it," Ed chides her in a friendly way. "I think they all die in the end."

"Huh?"

"Hey, Mr. Silent K," Andre says. "You got an innie or an outie?"

"My mom got a tramp stamp," Jake says. "Want to see a picture?"

"Are blue-balls really blue?" Andre asks.

"Put your phone away," Ed says.

"Can I go to the Nurse?" Andre asks.

"Why?" Ed says. "Did you eat the special?"

"Huh? No. My boys in the hood hurt."

"Mr. Silent K," Fowler says. "How old do you have to be to get a driver's license?"

"I don't know for sure. Sixteen?"

"See, Jake," Fowler says. "You got to wait two more years."

"Wait," Ed says. "Jake, your fourteen? Why are you in sixth—oh, never mind."

"Where's Mikey?" Ed asks no one in particular. "I thought I saw him this morning."

"In the office," Amy answers. "He bit Miss Vega."

"What! Where?"

"In math class."

"I mean *where* did he bite her?"

"In *math class.*"

"Never mind."

For the first time ever, the teachers think lunchtime is *too* long.

Kilo and Ed spend time together during planning.

"Did you come up with a catch-phrase yet? Maybe two? The kids love it, and it's a great way to bond. And sometimes you'll hear *them* use it."

"I haven't thought about that. What's yours?" Ed asks.

"They've evolved over the years. Right now, I'm using, 'What the crickets?'"

"I don't get it."

"Good! It needs to be whimsical, mysterious, and silly. 'What the crickets' is a mash-up of what the *heck* and *crickets*, as in 'Jiminy Cricket.'"

"What about, 'Oh my!'" Ed asks.

"No good."

"But, let me do the voice. George Takei. Listen again. 'OH MY!' They use it all the time on Howard Stern."

"That doesn't work either. It has to be original."

"How about 'Sammy Sosa?'"

"What does he say?"

"No, I have a friend and when she gets mad, instead of swearing, she says 'Sammy Sosa!'"

"Why?"

"I don't know. If you say it right, it's kind of catchy."

"It's different but I guess it will work," Kilo says. "And try and say something positive and sincere, even when a student says something dumb."

"Oh. My."

As if Ed's day can't get any longer, Cutty asks for his help covering the last half of a class for a seventh-grade teacher who went home sick.

Ed goes to the room where Mrs. Rivalry has covered the first half of the class.

"What's that smell?" Ed asks immediately as he walks in.

"My guess is Mr. Pock's lunch *after* he ate it. Apparently, he threw-up in the trash can. Maintenance took it but it but the room still smells. You'll get used to it. Here's a note and some worksheets. Good luck." Whoosh. Rivalry is gone.

Any disruption gets kids crazy, and having another teacher come in, a rookie at that, causes more chaos. Ed tries to get them settled down.

"Alright, it looks like attendance wasn't taken," Ed fibs. "OK! Settle down so you can hear me. Paige? Paige Turner? Ann, Ann Droid? Anita? Anita Bath?" Only a couple of kids catch on, but at least things are calming down.

Ed continues. "Molly? Molly Cule? Justin, Justin Time? Max? Max E. Pad?" Finally, some laughs.

"Noah, Noah Fence?"

One not too bright kid says, "That list must be from another class."

This doesn't stop Ed. "Matt? Matt Trez? Joe, Joe King? Hugh Jass?" 'Dick Hertz' might not be appropriate, so he skips that one.

"Patty? Patty O'Furniture?" *How long can I keep this up*, he thinks?

"Ida, Ida Ho?" Lots of chuckles for that one.

"Harry, Harry Palms?"

'Eew!' says half the class.

"Jim? Jim Nassium? Ella, Ella Mint? Cliff Hanger, are you here?"

This seems to calm the group, no small feat at the end of the day. Ed passes out the worksheets he knows will probably not get completed; busy work never does. Time goes fairly quickly, and the class soon ends.

When the last bell of the day rings, several faculty members, including Ed, follow the students outside and watch the buses load and drive away. It's a warm, sunny fall afternoon.

"Beautiful day," Kwaji says to Ed.

"Beautiful *time* of day."

"Ha," says Kwaji. "That reminds me of the three things you never want to hear from a student."

"Go ahead, shoot," Ed says.

"Make that four things," Kwaji replies.

"Oops, sorry."

"Kidding," Kwaji says. "Number one, 'I forgot to take my medicine.'"

"That's great!"

"Number two. 'I had four donuts and a Coke for breakfast!'"

"Excellent."

"Number three, 'Someone threw-up on the bus and we all stepped in it.'"

"Classic. Hey, I really like that sweater vest you're wearing."

"Oh, thanks," Kwaji says.

"You can't even tell it's Kevlar!"

Chapter Eight

It's early October and Ed makes an offer on a house. It's a quick closing because the owner passed away. Ed is at the closing held at the law office of Mr. Bob Lily, Esq. The office is in Lily's large Victorian home on Main Street.

"This shouldn't take long," Lily says.

"Start signing on this top page. Everything is marked."

Ed is signing his way through a stack of papers. A large dog snoozes in the corner.

Lily, making small talk, asks, "So how do you like it out here? I imagine it's a lot different than New York City."

"It sure is," Ed says. "But I miss the salsa."

"What do you mean?"

"Oh, nothing," Ed says. "It's an old TV commercial. Done, I think. Hey, that looks like a nice dog. Is it a Lab?"

"It is. And it's yours."

"What?"

"You see, Ed, I handled Mrs. Hayes's estate. Sold the house, handled the will. Mrs. Hayes was very specific. She has no living relatives, so sell everything, the money goes to charity, the dog goes with the house."

"What!" Ed says again. "What do you mean the dog goes with the house?"

"Well, Gelato—"

"Gelato? What kind of name is *that*?"

"And he has a brother in town, Pupino—"

"What? Who was this lady, Pinocchio's mother?"

"And a sister named Vino—"

"Vino! OK, now I *know* you're joking."

"Well, anyway," Lily continues. "Gelato stays with the house. Period. She was very clear she wanted the dog taken care of. The other two dogs have homes. Gelato lived with her. It has to be that way. It's in the contract."

"I thought she died a month ago. Where's Gelato been?"

"Here. In my house. Mostly right in that same spot."

"But."

"Ed, you signed the papers."

"You mean that two-foot stack of stuff you just made me sign? I didn't see anything about a *dog.*"

"Did you read every page?"

"Of course not! But you're *my* lawyer!"

"Well, I was *her* lawyer first. I'll get his leash."

"You know, I work all day. How am I going to take care of a dog?"

"Well, the backyard at your new house is fenced in. And there's a doggie door. And Gelato is familiar with the house. It really shouldn't be a problem."

"But I never had a dog! Don't you have to feed them and stuff?"

"Oh, that reminds me. I have everything you need. Bed, snacks, water bowl, food. You're all set."

"But how much do you feed a brute like this?"

"There's a scooper in the food bag. A level cup in the morning and evening."

"I don't know about this," Ed says reluctantly.

"I never had a problem while he was here. He eats and then sleeps about twenty-two hours a day."

"How old is he?"

"About five. He' a good pup, trust me."

Ed feels like saying *I'll never trust you again* but decides it won't help. Lily and Ed load Gelato into his SUV.

Ed wants to call Anita on his way home and tell her he is bringing a dog home, a very large dog, until he moves out next week, but she is working. *At least I have a backyard fence, but Anita doesn't*, he thinks to himself. Oh boy. Every time Gelato needs to go out I'm going to have to take him on a leash.

Ed takes chicken out of the oven as Anita walks in.

"What's this?" she asks, when a big dog quickly comes to the door.

"Well, I was going to call you, but…"

"You're so cute! What's he doing here?"

"Well, he came with my house."

"He *what*?"

"I had the closing today and—"

"Oh, yes. How did that go?"

"I'll tell you while we eat."

"Yes, something smells good. Is this a bribe?"

"That reminds me. I'll tell you what I miss living out here in the boondocks."

"What's that?"

"Food! You remember you can find anything in the city. And here, there's *one* supermarket and a McDonalds! All the store sells is old, white people stuff. There's no Hispanic or Asian food aisle or any of that kind of stuff. And I saw some tube of meat or something called 'scrabble.' What the heck is that?"

"Harold loved it, and it's called 'Scrapple.' And he loved pork rinds."

"Uh. You're not helping. And the registers are like antiques, so the lines never move. They even have those cups that your change dumps into when you pay. Who uses cash anymore?"

"Gee," Anita observes, "you are on a roll."

"And what kind of name is 'Food Lion King?'"

"It's Food Lion."

"Ha! What a dumb name for human food."

"No, that would be Piggly Wiggly or Winn-Dixie."

"How do you know all this stuff?" Ed asks.

"Harold and I took a lot of drives here and in the south. You remember he was afraid of flying."

"Yeah, he was afraid of flying but ate pork rinds?"

"That does sound kind of odd. You got me there."

Ed plates the food and starts telling the story of the dog as they sit down to eat. Gelato is up and circling the table like a shark looking for food.

"I made Shake and Bake chicken. I figured I can't screw that up."

"Sounds great. I've never had your cooking before."

She cuts her piece of chicken and the plate fills up with blood.

"Ed, this is raw! And cold."

"What! I followed the directions exactly."

"Did you turn the oven on?"

"Of course. I'm not *that* dumb."

"Wait. Where did you get the chicken from?"

"Your freezer. Why?"

"Did you defrost it?"

"It doesn't say that on the directions!"

"You cooked frozen chicken?"

"Look at the box," Ed says. "'Shake and Bake. Preheat the oven to 400 and cook for thirty-five minutes.'"

"You have to defrost it!"

"It doesn't say that!"

"That's because everyone knows."

"You're the one always telling me that cooking is easy if you just follow the instructions! That's what I did! You know I'm not Betty Crock-pot. I'm eating it."

Ed cuts the piece on his plate, and blood runs out.

"OK. Maybe not. Mm, I think we have cereal or Kibble and Bits. I'll get the bowls."

"Yes. And please tell me again why there is a dog maneuvering his giant body under my table."

"It's a long story…"

On Saturday, Ed fills the small U-Haul truck while Anita entertains Gelato. Soon they all drive to Ed's new house, with Gelato riding with Anita. The two have become buddies, even though Anita had to rush home the few days he was left there alone to let him out, and then rush back to school. It was easier for her to schedule it because of her autonomy, rather than Ed trying to sneak out of school.

When they turn down Ed's street, Gelato perks up like he knows where he's going. They put him in the backyard and move Ed into his new house.

"I'm getting too old for this," Anita complains. "Some of this stuff is *heavy*."

As it gets dark, Ed and Anita sit on Ed's one couch. Anita reluctantly drinks a beer as Ed has no idea what box the wine bottle opener is in.

"I've been meaning to ask you, Sis. What's up with this Nurse Atlas again? She seems like a real bully. How did she get hired?"

"Well, first of all, there aren't a lot of people lining up to be a school nurse, and not just here but all over the country. Not like in the old days. Remember Nurse Mahoney at PS-145?"

"She was great," Ed replies. "The white uniform, white shoes, the clinic. I bet she could cure cancer!"

"Well, nowadays nurses have a completely different role. Most of their time is spent making sure kids get their medicine and take it. Plus, in our school, we have a few kids with diabetes, so our nurse has to monitor their blood sugar and watch and make sure they inject themselves at the right time. And then there are kids with allergies. Between the kids and the nurse, there is a stack of epi-pens. And of course, daily vomiters."

"When did all this stuff start? That doesn't sound like a nurse; more like a health inspector!"

"No kidding. Then they have to be involved if anyone bleeds and watch for air-borne pathogens—"

"Why would anyone want that job?"

"That's my point. And they make about half what a hospital nurse makes because of budget cuts. And they have to deal with kids all day. The only selling point is again, short days and summers off."

"So, Nurse Atlas is new?"

"No. She's been there forever. She can't get hired anywhere else because of her charming personality. But honestly, I wish I had hired her."

"Wait," Ed counters. "You make it sound like she's a disaster!"

"She is, but in a *good* way."

"Explain. The only thing she seems to do in our school is stalk around with Derry."

"There's a hidden value to being nasty. She is this tall, hefty, bitter oaf. The Nurse's office is always empty. Kids are afraid of her; adults are afraid of her. A kid could break his arm in P.E. and plead not to go to the nurse. She's perfect!"

"The perfect *storm*," Ed retorts.

"No," Anita says. "Her and *Derry* are the perfect storm."

Suddenly, Gelato jumps between them on the couch. They both have to skootch over a bit so the eighty-pound dog can stretch out.

"He really is a good boy, aren't you Gelato?" Anita says.

"His name is no longer Gelato."

"You changed it?"

"My dog, my name."

"To what?"

"Savvy."

"Savvy? For a dog's name?"

"Hey," Ed replies. "I use it all the time in class for 'understand?' I like to teach the kids new words. And don't forget, your buddy says it a lot."

"My buddy? Who?"

"Captain Jack Sparrow."

"Oh, yeah, you're right."

"Anyway, take another look around while I finish the chicken."

"Oh, boy."

"Don't worry! This is *real* chicken, a whole chicken, and never frozen. Chicken, take two."

"But back to Derry. I guess I'm still on double-secret-probation."

"I told you there's no such thing. And Cutty really likes you. We have a principal's meeting almost every Wednesday and she told me you are doing great things. She also said you and Kilo are 'thick as thieves,' which she is fine with."

"Yeah, he helps me every day."

They have a nice meal and Anita heads home. With his bed and frame put together, Ed lies down, and almost immediately Savvy joins him.

"At least give me some blanket!" Ed complains.

Chapter Nine

Chorus class is an elective, though some random kids end up in there as well. Ms. Bostwick uses her strong personality to keep her students in line. She claps her hands for attention.

"Listen up! Our fall Contribution Program has been approved. I am happy to tell you that just like last year, we will be selling Famous Ernie's desserts. Cakes and eclairs and such. Like last year, they will be delivered to the school the Monday before Thanksgiving; perfect for family dinners.

"I know there were some complaints last year that these are unhealthy and too expensive, but they sell. Period. Last year we met our goal of five-hundred pieces. Your hard work brought in over two-thousand dollars. This year our goal is seven-hundred pieces, a couple more per student. You can do it!"

Students moan in unison, emitting frustration at the burden placed on them.

"Don't forget the teachers," Bostwick reminds the kids. "They are some of our best customers."

The next day in homeroom, Logan tentatively approaches her teacher, Mr. Silent K.

"Hi Mr. Silent K."

"Good morning, Logan. I like your sweater."

"Mr. Silent K?"

"Yes?"

Logan is opening her backpack.

"I'm trying to sell—"

The bell rings. Logan stuffs the Famous Ernie's catalogs back into her backpack but keeps one out.

"Homeroom has started," Mr. Silent K says. "Let's get going!"

"Um, I'll talk to you later," Logan says. "I wanted to know if you want to buy some choir food."

Logan leaves a catalog on his desk.

Ed is standing at the door as his homeroom students leave after the morning announcements and pledge of allegiance and his first class of students start to arrive.

"Good morning," he repeats several times.

A girl, named Vanity looks sad.

"What's wrong, Vanity?"

"I'm having a bad day."

"Why?"

"I don't know, it hasn't happened yet."

"So, you mean you are *going* to have a bad day."

"I am? Ugh, I knew it."

"No," Ed says, a little confused, but Vanity has moved on to her desk.

"Hey Mr. Silent K," Brandon yells from the back of the room. "You got a band-aid?"

"You want a new one or a used one?"

"Huh?"

"I've got one that was barely used. It just has a little puss on it."

"Eew! Never mind. Wait, what's *puss*?"

"Alright, let's get started. The warm-up question is on the board." Ed gives Brandon a new band-aid.

"Hey, Mr. Silent K," a student named Austin says. "I saw a picture of the space shuttle stuck on top of a big plane. Is that how little planes are made?"

"Ask your science teacher."

During lunch, Logan stays behind to try and sell her wares, overpriced globs of sugar, and items like cakes and things. Ed gives her forty-five dollars for three desserts, complaining the whole time about the high prices.

The next day, while on lunch duty, Logan brings the forty-five dollars back to Ed. She explains they can only take checks, not cash. Nurse Atlas is watching the transaction. She walks immediately to Derry's office and waits impatiently for him and hovers, waiting for him to get off the phone with a parent.

"What's so important?" he asks.

"I just saw a student, a *child,* buy drugs from your buddy Knudknickovich."

"What! Who? When? Where? What? Are you sure? Tell me exactly what you saw."

"I *just* saw it. I came right to your office. It was Logan Click."

"You saw drugs?"

"Well, not *exactly.* But what else could it be? She handed him a wad of cash for no reason."

"I don't know," Derry says. "But this is serious. I have to think about this one. The cafeteria cameras are terrible. I have to take your word."

"I know. We have to catch them."

"You mean stop them."

"Oh. OK. Catch them and stop them."

"Noooo. We have to *prevent* this."

"Well, we can figure that out later."

"You're right. First things first. We need to get Officer Goodwell, the SRO."

"No! She'll tell the police."

"She *is* the police."

"Yes, but we can't let them know yet. We need to catch, er, stop them before it happens."

"What do you mean?" Derry asks.

"We need more information," says Nurse Atlas. "Details. We need to follow them. If we confront them now, and they deny it, we have nothing but a bunch of trouble. Terry, we have to wait. Who better than us to get the details?"

"And it's Logan? I know the family. I know what happened to her father. I always thought she was a good kid."

"Even good kids can go bad trying to cope with something like losing a parent. Here's what I think we should do…"

Ed greets his students the next morning.

Logan asks him, "Mr. Silent K. Do you have the check?"

"I do. Here's a check for forty-five dollars. The eclairs must be gold-plated."

"Thank you. I can give you a receipt during lunch."

Homeroom ends and classes switch. Atlas hurries to get out of the way from looking in the door. She sees Logan with a folded piece of paper as she puts it in her pocket. Pills? A powder, maybe meth? After school the schemers' scheme. Atlas is somehow squeezed behind the wheel of her beat-up Saturn and Derry is nodding off in the passenger seat. They are parked across the street and down a few houses from Ed's new home. The plan is to spend the late afternoon following him. Will he meet his dealer? Or sell more drugs to kids?

"Wake up!" Atlas says.

"What the. Did you just elbow me?"

"Shh! He's leaving the house. Get ready. And write down the time."

Ed, unaware of being tailed, heads out to his first guitar lesson. He found the phone number on the community bulletin board in the supermarket, one of those little tear-off strips of paper. A longtime desire to master the instrument motivates him to try this stranger. Atlas and Derry follow, but not too closely.

When Ed arrives at the house of the woman he spoke to on the phone, he pops the back door and gets his guitar and case.

"Look!" Atlas says, her car parked way down the street. "He must carry the drugs in that guitar case.

"Put that camera away. I don't want neighbors wondering what we're doing."

"It's just in case. Plus, I can see better with the lens. The door is opening."

"I can *see* that myself," Terry Derry replies. "Oh, my God!"

"Oh, my God!" Atlas echoes Derry. They are flabbergasted at what they see.

"Oh, my goodness," Ed says when Logan Click opens the door. "Logan!"

"Mr. Silent K!" They both say, "What are you doing here?" at the same time.

Derry and Atlas are shocked to see Logan Click at the door as Atlas moves her car a little closer.

"What is *Logan* doing here?" Derry wonders.

"I told you. I told you. I *knew* it!" Atlas exclaims.

Ed says to Logan, "I have a guitar lesson. Maybe I wrote down the wrong directions."

"My mom is waiting for someone. Maybe it's you? I'll go get her. Don't let the dog get past you. Pupino! Stay!"

"Wait, Pupino! I've heard of this dog."

"Come in," Mrs. Click, a slim, medium height and very attractive woman says, coming up behind Logan.

"I'm Heather Click. We spoke on the phone. Wait, aren't you one of Logan's teachers? I've seen you at school. Mr. Silent K?"

"Actually, it's Ed, Ed Knudknickovich. Mr. Silent K is what the kids call me, right Logan?"

"Yeah. His name is like a mile long."

"I'm Logan's history teacher. The name Mr. Silent K is a long story."

"And homeroom," Logan adds.

"Well, again, come on in," Mrs. Click says.

"This is it," Atlas whispers to Derry as they walk up the driveway.

Right after closing the door, the Clicks hear a knock.

"That's odd," Mrs. Click says. "I hope I didn't book two people for lessons at the same time. I'm not sure who this is." She opens the door.

"Nurse Atlas. Hi. Was I expecting you? And Vice Principal Derry. Is Logan in some kind of trouble?"

"Mrs. Click," Nurse Atlas says, unsure of how to proceed now. "Um, well, you see, we are in the process of, um, well, Logan might be missing her T-Dap shot. Some of our paperwork got lost."

Ed is standing at the door as well, wearing a large frown.

"Mr. Derry, he's helping, in case we end up in a seedy neighborhood. We are out tracking down parents of kids we don't have the paperwork for. Not that this is a seedy neighborhood. In fact, you have a nice house. And what a pretty dog. Well, we'll be leaving now."

"The D-Tap," Mrs. Click says. "Logan got it over the summer."

"Oh, right, right. Good," Atlas responds. "Yes, that's great. Oh, hi Mr. Knudknickovich. I didn't see you back there. Well, we're all set! Sorry to bother you."

"Now *that* was odd," Mrs. Click says to the two people with her inside the house.

Derry and Atlas return to her car, arguing the entire way back to school.

"I'm your *helper*," Derry says.

"At least give me credit for saying *something*. You stood there like a stickman."

"Oh," Derry replies. "I should have said we think your daughter is a druggie? That was embarrassing enough. But

I'm going to get that Knudknickovich if it's the last thing I do."

"You mean *we* are."

Derry doesn't respond.

Ed's first guitar lesson is not going well.

"Ugh," a frustrated Ed says. "I've tried to learn the guitar about twenty times. My brain talks to my fingers, but they forget what to do before they move."

"Well, now you know how it is. I mean, as a teacher, when a student struggles."

"You know, in the spirit of full disclosure, I'm not really a teacher."

"Oh? I don't understand."

"I'm a teacher *now,* but I'm a career transitionary, so I just started this year. I took a bunch of classes and tests last year to get certified. My sister, Anita, really got me interested in teaching, and I have to say I am feeling a sense of fulfillment already. She's the principal at the high school."

"Anita Gold? I've met her. I didn't know you were her brother! I'm sorry to hear about her husband."

"Yeah, that's kind of why I'm here. She got the ball rolling for me. It's another long story."

"Well, if your teaching now, then you know all the buzzwords like differentiation, learning inventories, and Bloom's Taxonomy."

"Um, sure. But how do *you* know all this stuff?"

"I taught at the elementary school for a few years," Heather explains. "Second grade. I left when my husband died."

"Oh, sorry."

"It's OK. It was a while ago, over four years now. He died in Afghanistan. You know how they say, 'Time heals all wounds?' Don't believe them. Especially for my kids. That's why I left teaching, to be home more."

"Sorry, I didn't know. It must be really tough on Logan and?"

"Alex, her little brother. But, let's get back to the lesson. Now you know what it feels like as a struggling student when you don't get it. It's easy to shut down, get mad, or quit trying. That's when you earn your pay. A lot of times they are just trying to get your attention, and negative attention is better than none."

"Yes, teaching is tougher than I thought."

"It's never easy," Heather says. "Between parent apathy, student behavior, bureaucracy, budget cuts, and low pay."

"Now you sound like my sister. Believe me, I'm learning."

"Well, good for you for making this move. I think it's very admirable. And, I think schools could use more teachers with outside experience. Some have obviously lost their drive."

"It's the yelling that bothers me. I'm determined to never do it. First, I've never seen a situation *de-escalate* by yelling. And I got yelled at a lot in school. I just think it doesn't help, but I hear it when walking around. It certainly turned *me* off as a student."

"Then today's lesson should be cathartic. You have to find a way to *motivate* about what, a hundred students? And they all learn differently. One size does *not* fit all. Gee," Heather notes.

"I'm so sorry to lecture you. Between the interruption and the talking, our time is up. I have to get the kids working on their homework. I won't charge for this one. In fact, I've enjoyed our conversation. Now, do you want to keep this time slot, the same day and time?"

"I do."

"Good! And next time we will play guitar at your guitar lesson."

They part as more than acquaintances. There is a little 'flirt' in the air as Ed leaves, smiling.

Chapter Ten

It is Ed's, aka Mr. Silent K's, time to meet his requirement to observe another teacher's lesson. He picks one of Kilo Jones's science classes. He sees many of his own students. Ms. Rivalry covers Ed's class by taking them to the library.

"Alright," Kilo begins as Ed finds a seat in the back of the room and gets ready to fill out the observation form. "Good and bad things about alternative energy sources. We've talked about solar and wind. What's another? OK, clue. It involves water."

Amy says, "Rain?"

"Is that a question or an answer?"

"Well, there was that guy with the kite in a storm and he got hit by lightning and invented the light bulb."

"I'm not sure where to start with that one."

"Well, that's what we learned in second grade," Amy responds.

"Third grade," Fowler says.

Ed smiles. Typical. What grade it was in is more important than the actual topic.

"OK. Back on track," Kilo says. "So, we have a kite and lightning. Does that mean when you want to play a video game on your computer or TV you have to wait for a storm and plug it into lightning? Not exactly, of course. We need electricity. We want to generate electricity using water. Keyword *water*. Anyone else? Remember, there are no wrong answers unless you are not right. No takers?" Kilo asks.

There is an awkward silence.

"Well, let me get my *People* magazine while we wait."

Ed is impressed that Kilo has no problem waiting for an answer and lets the silence linger. Ed watches intently how Kilo patiently generates participation from the kids.

"I'll try," Fowler finally says.

"Great! A volunteer. Go ahead."

"I saw on the Discovery Channel where there was a river, I think it was in China, and they blocked it off but I'm not sure how they got the electricity out. I think it was called hypo-something. I think they built a dam, too."

"Excellent. And Fowler, they aren't laughing at you. The *children* are laughing because you said dam. Fowler, you are absolutely, one hundred percent almost right. It's called *hydroelectricity*. We already know what 'hydro' means, right Andre?"

"Oh, me? Um, I know this one, wait. What was the question?"

Kilo moves his hands to imitate rain falling.

"I got this," Andre exclaims. "Jazz hands!"

Kilo steps closer to the young man until he is right in front of him.

"OK, OK. Rain, er water."

"Correct. 'Hydro' means water. So hydroelectricity is generated by water, *moving* water. And like any alternative source of energy, anything that is *not* a fossil fuel, there is good and bad. Solar on a cloudy day, no good. Windmills with no wind, no good. For water, it's best told with a story. Let's say there's a river."

Kilo is drawing with a marker on the whiteboard.

"What happens is, they dam off the river with a really tall dam, and kind of funnel the water into these tubes that spin turbines. Now once they block off the river, the water backs up into a huge lake to ensure the water is flowing quickly through the tubes. If anyone used to live there, they move out before the water backs up. They buy their houses and clear everyone out."

Kilo continues to illustrate on the board. A bunch of hands go up.

"I know what you are going to ask. What if they don't want to move? How much money do they get? How do you build a dam when the river water is moving? Right. Well, I have a quick video that shows the whole process. Any other questions so far? Logan, you look perplexed."

"I feel OK."

"No. It's not a disease. It means confused, or inquisitive. Did you have a different question?"

"Yes," Logan replies.

"Go ahead."

"Well, I was just wondering, you know, if they move the people, the people that live there, because it's underwater..."

"Yes?"

"What do they do with the animals?"

"What animals?"

"Not cats and dogs. People probably take them with them," Logan deduces.

"Yes'?"

"I mean the *other* animals, the ones that live outside."

"Yes?"

"Deer and skunks and stuff."

"Yes?"

"What happens to them?"

"Great question! And that's what my story is about. The government or the power company or someone helps people relocate. Seems fair, right? They can say this land around the river is better used for thousands of people, for nearby homes or farms to get electricity. But the animals. What about the animals? The lions and tigers and bears, oh my. And the deer and skunks. And squirrels. What happens to them?"

Kilo is now walking around, ready to engage the imaginations of the young minds in the room. Ed has been sucked in as well.

"Let's say there is a big river near the woods. It's been there forever. It's a haven for wildlife; all the animals we mentioned. One day they start to hear trucks and construction and humans talking. It's loud and it lasts for years. And all of the people that lived there are gone. And the river, the animal's source of water and a necessary ingredient for life, is doing strange things. The river seems to move faster, and then slower, then wider, then narrower. What the heck are these crazy humans up to?"

Kilo pauses for effect.

"So, life goes on. Then one day, early in the morning, the animals are alerted by a strange sound. They freeze. They listen. Something is happening. This is when the dam is finished to make a lake behind it.

"Four deer come charging through a clearing. 'Run! Run for your lives,' they shout. And they're gone so quickly nobody hesitates to even ask what is happening. Everybody, everything, runs. The deer are lopping, and the bunnies are hopping, and the squirrels are bounding, and the ducks are ducking. *Flood!* Their land, their homes, the rushing water. What's going on? The river's gone crazy! Ruuuuunnnnnn!"

Kilo is getting animated in front of his completely engaged students.

"Families are trying to stay together. The deer are lopping, and the bunnies are—wait! Grandpa Rabbit has stopped! 'Leave me,' he says. 'I'm weak, I'm old,' he says quickly, out of breath. His daughter goes to him. 'Pa.' Get it? 'Pa, we can't leave you!' There are tears in her eyes."

"'Go,' he yells. 'Save yourselves! This is the only home I've ever known. I'm staying…'"

"The daughter hesitates, then runs and yells to the rest, glancing back one more time to see her Pa sitting on his favorite tree stump, looking very old, facing the end bravely. And the deer are lopping, and the bunnies are hopping, and the squirrels are bounding."

"'Higher ground!' a deer, the fastest animals, yells. Everything is running for their life. 'Up ahead,' says the deer. 'Higher ground! An embankment! We can make it!' And the deer are lopping, and the bunnies are hopping, and the squirrels are bounding.'"

The children are hushed, mesmerized by the story.

"The deer jump the ridge first, then the rabbits, squirrels, and ducks oh my. Wait! The other side of the hill is a highway! Trucks! Cars! Fur goes flying! Splat! Splat! Deer are bouncing off windshields, rabbits are being run over, squirrels are squished under tires! Body parts are flying in every direction! Cars swerve covered in blood. It's all gone terribly wrong."

There is dead silence in the room. Ed looks around from his seat in the back, waiting for someone to throw up. All the kids look pale. They are stunned.

"And that's what happens to the animals. And that's the bad part of hydroelectricity. The end. Now please draw my picture of the river and dam in your journal."

A nauseous Ed has completely forgotten to fill out the observation form. He will have to do it during planning. This was a story Ed and the kids would not forget. Maybe that was the point.

The noisy Teacher's Lounge is not much solace, except when Guy White starts to talk. He's at it again.

"I have this idea for all the English classes," Guy starts off innocently enough.

"I call it 'Literal Day.'"

"I'll bite," Kilo says, one of the few people who is entertained by Guy.

"You know how everyone overuses the word 'literally,' right? So, we have one day that everything people say we have to take literally. Example, you sneeze, and I say, 'Bless you.' And now I have to bless you!"

"But that's what 'Bless you' means," says Larkin.

"Alright. Different example. What if someone says, 'We have to draw straws.' Everyone would have to take out a paper and pencil and draw a straw. Get it?"

"I think it needs some work…" Kwaji says.

Guy continues. "But there's so many more! 'Don't go there,' so you can't; 'bite me,' so you have to; 'come on, hop to it,' so you hop.'"

"And what's the point?" Ed asks.

"To make people realize how often they say things like clichés and stuff, and overuse 'literally' all the time. It's so annoying it makes me want to puke."

"Uh-oh," Ed says to Guy. "You have to puke."

"Yeah," Kilo adds. "Guy, knock yourself out."

Chapter Eleven

Parent-Teacher conferences are tonight. Ed feels nervous. He wants to make a good impression and figures Derry will be watching to hope he fails. Ed is a little groggy from a restless night, which included an odd dream. When he walked into his classroom, it was full of parents, but they were all cartoon characters! Fred and Wilma Flintstone in the front row. Homer and Marge Simpson, George and Judy Jetson, Hank and Peggy Hill, and Peter and Lois Griffin were there, sitting next to Sherman and Peabody.

Ed seeks encouragement from his mentor, Kilo.

"So, Kilo, are you ready for tonight?"

"Why, what's tonight?"

"Parent-Teacher conferences. My first one!"

"Oh, yeah. You'll do fine. Make sure you have your grades and have some example papers and quizzes to show for any failing kids so the parents can see the kind of work they are doing. But you never know which parents are going to be aggressive. Just end by looking them in the eye, tell them they have a fine son or daughter and you feel lucky to have them in your class. Doesn't matter what you really think."

"That's it? Thanks for the heads-up."

"No wisdom," Kilo says confidently. "It's just like everything else. Tell people what they want to hear and play nice. Two more things. Watch out for the parents of the kids with an A. Their child can have a ninety-nine percent average and they'll complain it's not a hundred."

"And?"

"*Always* remember you are talking about someone's child. Parents get very defensive about everything and anything when it comes to their perfect children."

"Good to know."

"And third, there's always one or two parents that will call you by your first name. It's an intimidation tactic. Don't react. That's what they want."

"Crap," he replies. "It's almost six. I have to get ready. I'm going to change my shirt and tie and do a quick shave. I'll see you later."

Ed is in the Boy's Room where there is much more space than the Teacher's bathroom.

He hears a noise and turns around. It's Fowler.

"Mr. Silent K? Are you shaving? Do you *live* here?"

"What? No, of course not. I live in my car. I just use the bathroom here."

"Really?"

"No. I'm just kidding."

"Oh, I thought you lived here with Mr. Larkin."

"Nope. Mr. Larkin?"

Nurse Atlas is lurking outside the door-less bathroom, listening to male voices.

"Hey, Mr. Silent K," Fowler continues. "How come there are no showers in this school? We have P.E. but we can't shower. I wonder if they have showers in high school. I think they do because I heard you *have* to shower."

"Not sure," Ed says. "I heard there used to be showers here but they tore them out, or don't use them anymore."

"Why not?"

"How would I. I mean I'm new, so I really don't know. Why are you here, anyway?"

"I have to take a leak. I'm a helper. We help parents find classrooms and answer questions and stuff. There's a bunch of us. You have to be an honor student to get picked."

"Oh. Good for you! Are you early?"

"Yeah. My parents dropped me off and went to dinner. Still, I'm not showering with other boys."

"Don't blame ya.'"

Nurse Atlas bursts in!

"Who is in here? No one should be here yet. Why are you talking about showering with boys? Oh, Mr. Knudknickovich. I heard voices."

"Nurse Atlas!" Fowler exclaims. "What are you doing in the *Boy's Room?*"

Ed jumps into the conversation.

"Yeah, Nurse Atlas. What are you doing in here?"

"Just looking for, er, just checking that things are tip-top, tip-top."

Conferences are ready to start, and Ed is back in his classroom with the schedule of when parents will arrive.

"Mrs. Wily? Come on in. Oh, Amy, too. I didn't know you were coming. Come in and sit down."

"My husband was supposed to be here but he's sick. So he says. He stayed home with the baby but I travel eighty percent of the time; I'm almost never home. I just can't believe Amy has a B in social studies, or history, or whatever it's called now. How hard can it be? And it's not like it's important."

"OK," Ed replies. "This paper shows Amy's grade on each assignment and test. It's available on the school's website. You can create a personal password and—"

"I *told* you. My husband does all of this stuff. *He* isn't working. He doesn't travel. Besides, isn't it *your* job to make sure she does well on tests? And what are all these zeros?"

"Those are missing homework assignments. They can be made up and—"

"You're not doing your homework?" Mrs. Wily chastises Amy.

"I did them but didn't hand them in."

"Your father is *supposed* to be checking your homework. I work; he doesn't. Ed, aren't you making sure the kids are doing their homework? What's going on?"

Ed hesitates and decides not to tell Mrs. Wily it is both the parent's *and* the student's responsibility to get the homework done. Ten more minutes drag by. Amy is clearly embarrassed by her mother's behavior and how she is berating her father and Mr. Silent K. Mrs. Wily finally gets ready to leave.

"I expect to see improvement," Mrs. Wily says to Ed and drags Amy out the door.

A few more parents come and go. The last conference of the evening is about Andre.

A minute later Ed is greeting Mrs. Martinez, Andre's mother.

"Hello, Mrs. Martinez."

"Good evening. It's nice to meet you. I hear your name once in a while."

"Please," Ed says. "Take a seat."

Mrs. Martinez wastes no time.

"I'll get right to it. Andre's father is in Maryland. He runs the grill at Chilis. It pays more than here. Before that, well, he wasn't around much. Andre could probably go live with him but it's not a good environment. Trust me. Andre needs direction, discipline. I've seen his bad side and I don't like it. He's better off with me, so that makes you his male role model. See, after his mom passed away—"

"Oh! I thought *you* were his mom."

"I'm his grandmother. His mother's mother. Sorry. I guess I didn't say that. His mom died four-and-half years ago. Cancer."

"I see."

"He likes you. He says you talk to him. Not everybody does in this school. He's just one of those kids it's easy to ignore unless he's causing trouble. He brought a reputation from elementary school. They actually held him back a year rather than try and help him. I don't want him to be pushed through middle school just to get rid of him. But you, he says you talk to him. More importantly, he says you *listen* to him. Seems pretty simple to me. A teacher talking and listening to kids, *all* kids, but I guess it doesn't happen much anymore. And this school, this area, is not very diverse."

"I've noticed that. And I try and get to everybody."

"He even tells me once in a while he wants to be a teacher. Used to be he wanted to grow up and be a football player, like every other kid. Before that he wanted to be a *NCIS,* whatever was big on TV."

"Now," Ed interjects, "all the kids want to design video games or be YouTube stars."

"I don't even know what that means. Anyway, we're in this together. I need your help and I'm not afraid to ask. My one-shot. I want everything I can get for him. He's not dumb but he's treated that way. His education is all he's got."

"I'm on board," Ed says sincerely. "And I'll talk to Mr. Jones as well, his science teacher. We all want the same thing."

"How come there are so few men teachers here? He didn't have any in elementary school."

"I've noticed the same thing. I'm one of maybe five. I don't have an answer for you."

"Well, I feel good about you based on Andre's comments. And that's a compliment I haven't been able to say very often. And you seem to have figured out he doesn't respond well to yelling or being chastised. Not that anyone does."

"I agree. And I feel like I have a pretty good rapport with him."

"Good. And maybe you can help him with his state test scores. He's never passed a single one, not any subject. That's another bad label he has."

"I'll do everything I can. I promise. Andre is a good kid once you get to know him."

Ed and Mrs. Martinez exchange pleasantries as she leaves. Ed is beginning to feel like a real teacher!

Kilo walks into Ed's classroom.

"So?" he asks.

"It was good," Ed says. "Just odd. One parent blamed me for everything wrong, and Andre's grandmother complimented me."

"Welcome to the world of education. Some parents want you to be a babysitter, and some realize your value. It's about fifty-fifty. Funny, I just saw a cartoon I meant to bring in, a drawing. The bottom says '1960s' and there is a teacher behind the desk, a student in front of the desk holding a paper with an F on it, and both the parents and teacher says to the kid, 'What are you doing about this?' Then next to it is the same scene, but it says, '2000s' at the bottom with the same people in the room. But this time when the kid holds up an F, he and the parents say to the teacher, 'What are *you* doing about this?' Talk about change!"

"You should bring it in and hang it somewhere, like the teacher's lounge."

"I don't want to add to any negativity. Society has changed the rules; we have to change, too."

"That makes sense."

"OK, well, Public Ed, I'm leaving. See you back in a few hours."

"Good night."

It is now 8:45 and Ed is packing up to go home. He walks past the boy's room and hears a noise. He enters and freezes. Mr. Larkin is wearing a bathrobe and is brushing his teeth in one of the small sinks. Ed tries to slink away.

"Eddie, old boy," Larkin says.

"Mr. Larkin!"

"It's George, my young friend."

"I was just leaving," Ed says.

"I'll walk with you," Larkin replies. "Let me put my things in the duffel. There we go."

"Mr. Larkin?"

"George."

"Right, George. Is everything all right?"

"Do you have time for a story, Eddie?"

"Sure, but don't they lock up soon?"

"The custodians always give a five-minute warning on the P.A. Come to my room."

Ed and George enter Larkin's classroom.

"Look, Eddie. A bit awkward, ay? This is temporary and I hope our little secret. I lost my home, Eddie. Foreclosed."

"When?"

"November the first. Bad day."

"I'm sorry!" Ed replies.

"It's a lesson. I'm sure no one wants to be broke at sixty-three. Paycheck to paycheck, tough to save. I'll be back on my feet soon. Don't pity me, though. Most of my money went to my granddaughter's college education. And hey, this is quite an adventure! Reminds me of *Oliver Twist.* Have you read it, Eddie?"

"What? Oh, yes. But nobody knows?"

"Oh sure, Eddie. It's a classic! Dickens' second novel. We read a chapter a week out loud in my classes."

"No. Does anybody know you're here?"

"Not a soul. Present company excluded."

Ed is thinking back to Fowler saying something about Larkin. The night custodian cuts in on the P.A.

"Anybody left? The fat guy is going to start singing!"

"He means it. Hurry Eddie, you don't want to get locked in. We'll talk tomorrow."

"Good night."

The custodian lets Ed out the front door.

"Good night," he says to Ed. *But was it,* Ed thinks, *shocked about Larkin?*

The next day, Ed has an eye doctor appointment. He is going during his planning. He passes Miss Vega and says he'll be back before the buses load. He senses something is up.

"Is something wrong?" he asks.

"I'm getting *really* aggravated. I better not have *one more person* ask me if I'm a student! It kept happening again last night!"

"Well, you are petite. And you do look about fourteen. Hey, what is that toy watch you're wearing?"

"It's a Fit-Bit. I'm tracking how many steps I walk each day."

"You know there's an app for that," Ed explains to the young teacher. "You can track the same thing on your phone. I tried it but my foot was killing me."

"What? Why?"

"You have to keep your phone in your shoe."

"Ugh. Why do I listen to you? Don't you have an appointment somewhere?"

"Oh yeah, the doctor. I'm on a shortlist for an appendix transplant."

"Really? Are you serious?"

Ed shakes his head 'yes' and then says, "No."

"Wait. What? Oh, you're a dumbass. Oops." She looks around to see if any kids might have heard her in the hallway, but it's empty.

"Potty mouth! I'm going to the eye doctor. I'll be back as soon as I can. It was the only appointment I could get. Are you going to miss me?"

"No."

"Gee, I guess you didn't go to finishing school."

"I finished school! Now go, shoo…"

Nurse Atlas, vigilant as always, watches Ed leave. She keeps her eyes open for his return. Suspicion bubbles up when she sees him come back forty minutes later as he struggles to park and seems disoriented.

Miss Vega says, "Oh, good. You're back. Derry was looking for you."

"Really? Are you serious?"

"No. Hey, are you OK? You look a bit wobbly."

"I'm fine, except I can't see."

"Kind of defeats the purpose of going to the eye doctor."

"They gave me those drops. I think I'm still fully dilated, like ten-centimeters."

"Gross."

"Well, see you later, or not."

Nurse Atlas is in Derry's office.

"I'm telling you," she says to Derry. "He's drunk. Knudknickovich left for a while and he came back drunk!"

"Start over again. After our last trip, I'm not rushing into anything."

"He had trouble parking. He's stumbling. He must have been drinking. We *have* to test him."

"I heard you. But how? And what if we're wrong? And I need to talk to Cutty first."

"There are several ways. Urine, blood. I have kits in the clinic."

"I know *how*," Derry says. "I mean how are we going to do it? I can't just grab somebody and tell them to pee in a jar. I need grounds for that. And we don't have much time before everyone leaves."

Atlas is thinking, ever scheming.

"I've got it. TB!"

"TB?"

"Yes! We tell him we are testing the entire staff for tuberculosis and we need a blood test! We say the order came from the Board of Health."

"Well, I don't know. This is pretty risky."

"Come here," Atlas whispers. "I can see him at the copy machine."

Ed is at the copy machine in the middle of the office, fumbling through a simple chore.

"And go look at his pupils. They're the size of pancakes."

Derry gets up and watches.

"OK, we'll do this. Cutty is not here. She's at the principal's meeting, so I'll say I took the initiative."

Just then Cutty walks into the office. She sees Atlas and Derry.

"Good. You're both here. I came back early because it was reported that an elementary student might have the measles. This could present a major health issue with students and parents. I have a written communication plan and some steps we need to take immediately. Let's go!"

Atlas and Derry join Cutty, determined to get Knudknickovich another day. Ed finishes his copies and goes to find Kilo to talk about Larkin, but he's gone for the day.

It is a busy and unsettling time for Ed. The parent conferences went well. Meeting Heather Click was a blessing, and Ed can't help feeling the widow is quite attractive. Savvy is getting used to living with Ed, but Ed feels guilty he's home alone all day. And George Larkin. How can he help him? Ed has an idea.

Chapter Twelve

Ed's weekend is busy. He makes time to walk and throw a ball with Savvy and spends Sunday with Anita. He floats his idea about Larkin, and Anita agrees. Monday means back to school. Ed speaks to Kilo about Larkin and his predicament, even though he promised to keep it quiet.

"I have three bedrooms at my new house. It would be OK if he stayed with me, wouldn't it?" Ed asks.

"Sure. Teachers room together all the time, especially the new ones who have to split the rent because their salary won't cover a good lunch."

Ed plans to talk to Larkin after school.

Noontime finds Ed in the teacher's lounge after a fast-moving morning. Once again, Ed hears teachers swapping stories.

"What are you looking at?" Kilo says to Veronica Vega, who is holding what looks like a pamphlet.

"I got this in the mail. There's a math cruise this spring."

"That sounds exciting," Ed interjects. "Where does it go, the Bermuda *triangle*? Get it?"

"Yes, I get it," Veronica replies.

As usual, there are multiple conversations happening at the same time.

"It's not good," Ms. Rivalry tells her friend. "I think my mother has Crohn's disease."

Guy White butts in. "Chrome's disease? Does that turn your poop silver? Interesting…"

Miss Vega complains, "So then the kid says, 'How come you only yell at me when you hear me talking, but you never hear me when I'm *not* talking?' It makes no sense!"

Ed has a story. "I was handing out a crossword puzzle and someone asked if spelling counts! So, I'm licking my fingers to pass them out, you know how they stick together, and Blake says, 'Eew! I don't want your slobber on my paper.' She wanted a different one. I said you are getting a little snippy, and she says, 'I'm sure I don't know what that means. Now, can I have a new paper?'"

It's Miss Vega's turn again to speak at the table. "All my classes bombed the fractions test. Listen to this. When we were reviewing, I drew a shirt in a store on the board and said there's a sign next to it. One side says, 'Fifty percent off' and the other side says, 'Half off.' And before I can say anything Jake yells out, 'So which is it?' Ugh!"

"Sounds like they failed in epic *proportions*. Get it?" Ed asks. Veronica just rolls her eyes.

Time flies by, as usual. It really is the fastest time of the day. On the way back to get their students, Ed tells Kilo he is going to speak to Larkin that afternoon.

It's another beautiful late fall day. Leaves are falling everywhere with the breeze. Many teachers migrate outside as the buses load up. Ed finds himself next to Principal Cutty.

"So, Ed, or Mr. Silent K. Tell me, do you miss your old job?"

"Honestly? No. I still have friends in New York from work and stuff but I'm really starting to love teaching. Oh, there are a couple tough kids but I take it that is normal. But overall, I'm feeling very good about how things are going so far. I'm enjoying it, something that was lacking from my last job."

"Good to hear. And yes, there are always some challenging students. But even if you impact just a few, you could end up molding their life in a positive way. Look at the bond you have with Andre Martinez. I spoke to his grandmother really quick during conferences. Trust me, I know his background. The elementary school always gives us a list of 'challenging' students, but so far so good. And I credit you. You should feel great! You are making a difference."

"Thank you. I do feel good. There was very little job satisfaction in a room full of writers, but teaching. I'm glad I made the switch. Once in a while, I feel like a fish out of water, but so far, so good."

Kwaji is herding a group of late students out the door and to the buses. He says, "'So ye shall go out with joy and be led forth in peace.' Do any of you kids know who said that?"

A student answers, "Dr. Seuss?"

Another kid guesses, "Kanye?"

"Jesus Christ!" Kwaji exclaims.

The first student says, "Why are you so mad?"

The other kid says, "Yeah. Why are you yelling at us?"

"Never mind," Kwaji says. "Have a good day, fellas."

Kilo and Ed make time after school to talk about Larkin and finalize a plan. Kilo is still surprised to find out their colleague is homeless. They discuss it and figure out a way to help and how to address it with Larkin. Ed asks Kilo to come with him, anticipating Larkin might be too proud to accept.

The two double-team Larkin, who sits quietly as Ed proposes his idea of moving in with him until he gets back on his feet. Pride and independence are factors, but George acquiesces the offer. Kilo then talks to George about helping to look at his finances, thinking he might be able to help. Kilo and Ed say they would concoct a story if any teachers asked what was going on.

The era of George Larkin moving in takes place that very afternoon. Larkin loves dogs confirmed by allowing Savvy to lick him for five minutes. Kilo shows George his room that contains only a blow-up mattress.

"I've been meaning to get more furniture," Ed says, a little embarrassed. "I had a very small apartment in New York City, so this is all the furniture I have."

The two sit on the couch and share a beer with Savvy in the middle of the two men. The chatting ends and Ed starts to set up George with what he will need but discovers he has almost everything in his duffle bag.

"Good night, George," Ed says.

"Eddie, you have no idea how much I appreciate this," George says through misty eyes. "This is not how I expected to live my golden years."

A couple of hours later Ed rolls over and there is no Savvy on his bed. Turns out he spent the night lying next to George.

Kilo Jones brings his first class the next day to the library to work on their mini-research paper.

"Before I let you get started, let's cover this one more time. Logan, what is the name of the project?"

"My Favorite Planet."

"Excellent. Does everyone have the template? Fowler, do all of the lines need to be filled in?"

"Yes."

"Plus?" Kilo asks.

"Three additional facts," Fowler answers.

"Good. Questions? Andre?"

"Can I do mine on the moon?"

"You want to *work* on it on the moon, or you want to *write* about the moon?"

"Both!"

"Blake, will you please answer Andre?"

"The moon is not a planet. Gee!"

Jake asks, "Can I do mine about Earth?"

"Blake?"

"Yes, Earth is a planet. Duh!"

"Be nice."

Kilo strolls among the students sitting in groups of three and four at the round library tables. He is enjoying the whimsical chatter of eleven and twelve-year olds.

"Hey, Mr. Jones," Amy says. "Do you know about the Civil War?"

"You mean the United States Civil War?"

"I guess so. The one we have to learn about."

"Yes."

"Isn't it true the Asians lost it?"

"How's that?"

"The *Asians.* Didn't some General Lee surrender?"

"Oh, boy. What the Crickets?"

"Hey, Mr. Jones," Amy says. "What was that other thing you called oil last week? Some fancy word?"

Fowler jokes, "Oil of Olay?"

"Why would I want to know the Spanish word for it? No, it was like 'lapoleum' or something."

"Petroleum," Kilo answers.

"Yeah, why do they call it that?"

"Well, petroleum is a Latin word."

"Why is everything Latin?" Andre chimes in from another table. "You said they named the elements, too. Did they have their own words for everything or something?"

"OK. First, 'petra' means rock, and 'oleum' means oil. So, it means oil from rocks, actually *under* rocks. Now we usually just call it oil."

"That means petroleum jelly comes from under a rock? My mom is always putting it on my scabs and stuff," Austin adds.

Kilo says, "There are a lot of things that start as oil, and then it has to be refined. That means—"

"I know," says Not Bob. "It starts as oil, but then they separate it or add stuff to make other things, like gasoline."

"My momma's been rubbing gasoline on me?" Austin says to Kilo.

"I'm going to another table," Kilo says, sighing.

"Hi, Mr. Jones. You going to sit with us?"

"Sure. What is everyone working on?"

"I'm doing Mercury," Logan says.

"Why?" Kilo asks and holds his breath.

"Because it's the hottest planet since it's so close to the Sun."

"I thought you said Venus is the hottest?" Amy asks. "That's why they gave it a girl's name."

"OK, you're both almost right. What I *said* was they have different atmospheres. One holds heat and one lets it escape."

"Oh, yeah," Amy says. "You told us Venus has a blanket, and Mercury has a sheet with holes in it."

"That's right. Which would keep you warmer?"

"A blanket!" Amy answers.

"But you said *I* was right, too," Logan says.

"Well," Kilo answers the question that always stumps the kids. "Since Mercury is the closest to the Sun it *does* get hotter, but it can't hold it, so it is very cold at night. But on average, Venus is hotter."

"Isn't average the same as mean?" Fowler asks.

"You better ask your math teacher. I don't want to teach it differently."

"Why do teachers always say that?" Fowler inquires. "'Go ask your other teacher.' Aren't you all teachers?"

"Um, go ask another teacher."

Kilo goes to the next table.

"Hey, Mr. Jones," Andre says over his shoulder. "Not-Bob says cheese comes from cows. I say it comes from 7-11. Tell him he's wrong."

"What class do you have next?" Kilo asks Jake.

"P.E."

"No, we don't," Andre says. "We have gym."

"When is Mrs. Clanton having her baby?" Austin asks.

"I think about a month."

"That is going to be the smartest baby ever."

"Why?" Kilo asks hesitantly.

"Because it's in school every day!"

"Babies that aren't born yet can't hear nothing," Andre says. "They're in a big bubble of fat."

"They can, too! They can hear through their mom's bellybutton, isn't that right, Mr. Jones? Isn't that what it's for?"

"Well, that doesn't sound quite right…"

"You have kids, Mr. Jones?" Not-Bob asks as Kilo tries to escape.

"I don't."

"Well then you don't know for sure, do you."

Not-Bob then asks, "Hey, Mr. Jones. You ever heard of 'U-Haul?'"

"Sure. It's still owned by the family that started it a long time ago."

"Told ya,' Jake! Their last name is U-Haul."

I need to start writing this stuff down, Kilo thinks, hoping to look at the clock and see the class is almost over. No such luck.

It's after school and Kilo enters Ed's classroom.

"What's wrong, Public Ed?"

"I'm just feeling a little overwhelmed. I have papers to grade, a dog to walk, keep in good standing with Derry, who I'm sure is out to get me because he always looks angry, and this whole Larkin thing."

"Welcome to teaching."

A week later Derry is sitting with Ed in his classroom discussing lesson plans, and how to use project-based learning, his new hot button. The animosity exhibited so often by Derry seems to subside a little.

Derry starts the conversation.

"OK, this is going to be a large part of your Improvement Plan. I'm going to share an important learning strategy, and it's your job to implement it successfully. What you do is create an activity, actually a project, where the students have to create their own country starting with a blank sheet of paper."

Derry loosens his tie.

"Mm, that sounds interesting," Ed says, pleasantly surprised. He doesn't dare tell Derry that Kilo and he had some fun making *their* own country.

"They have to design everything from scratch. What kind of government, the economy, what do they produce, what do they have or not have as far as natural resources? Where is the country," Derry continues, "what continent? Is there a seacoast or is it landlocked? You see, by putting all of these categories on a rubric you are setting clear expectations for each student. But at the same time, they get to use their imagination, but include knowledge about the topic as well."

"Interesting."

"Let them use maps. Look at this wall map for example. There are so many things the students have to consider. Are our neighbors friendly or aggressive?"

"I like this idea, I do," Ed says sincerely. "But how does it tie into World War I, which is where we are on the curriculum guide?"

"This is a *project.* Students work on it over time. You keep teaching your topic and give them a little time each day to work on it."

Ed, in no position to challenge Derry, says, "OK. I'll make it work, even though I have students that think the Equator is the leader of the *Transformers.*"

"I don't understand," Derry says.

"Never mind." Ed forgot Derry seems to have no sense of humor.

"Here, let's grab some paper and sketch out a sample so the kids understand it better."

Ed gets up and brings over some paper, feeling Derry is almost friendly.

"Draw up a rubric, something like this," Derry says. "Two weeks, students check-in with you twice a week. You have a first, second, and third place ribbon for each class. Now, always give them a choice because they all learn differently. Call it a menu. They can do a written report, a diorama, a PowerPoint…"

Ed is paying close attention, thinking this is either a trick or a way to get on Derry's good side.

The next day, Ed is explaining Derry's project to his students.

"So, again. It's called 'My Country.' Questions?"

"I'll tell you what. Mine is going to be called Jake-Land. And I'm the King! And it's going to have palm trees, and babes—"

"This isn't an episode of *Gilligan's Island,*" Ed interjects.

"Who?"

"Jake, you're making me crazy. Let me finish and then I'll answer more questions. This is a fictional country based on—"

"What's frictional?" Jake asks.

"Can I get up and look at the globe?" Logan asks.

"Can I go to the bathroom?" Fowler asks.

"This pencil sharpener doesn't work," Andre says. "Why can't you get an electric one like Miss Vega?"

"Can I do mine about Atlantis?" Austin asks.

"Can I use a computer?" Logan asks.

"Everybody hold on and let me finish." Ed uses the screen to show a PowerPoint he created as an example to inspire the students. He explains each slide.

"I'm going to call mine 'K-A-Duh,'" Ed says. "Or 'Silent K-A-Duh.' It's populated with snowmen."

Ed continues his example of his country. An arm shoots up.

"Yes, Blake?"

"Can I show my presentation now?" At some point, she had snagged a laptop from the back table.

"Now?"

"It's done. I just finished."

"Well…"

"It's not due for two weeks!" Fowler exclaims, having returned from the Boy's Room and overhearing Blake.

"I didn't start yet!" Andre says.

"It was due today?" Not-Bob asks.

"OK, stop," Ed says. "One at a time. And Amy, please pass out the scoring rubric so we can go through it."

"Well?" Blake says, still waiting for an answer.

"You're going to have to wait. I'll look at it with you in a little while. Let's use the rest of today's class to work on your paper. We'll spend some time on this during each class for the next two weeks."

"What am I supposed to do until *then*?" over-achiever Blake asks.

"I'll be there in a minute."

Ed works the room to get the kids started, but kids will be kids.

"I'm telling you," Fowler says. "*Jurassic World* is right. Dinosaurs lay eggs."

"No," Andre says. "Birds lay eggs. And chickens. Dinosaurs popped those things out like puppies, like eight at a time."

"No," Fowler replies. "Birds and dinosaurs are reptiles. Look at pictures. Things without eggs don't have nipples."

"I'm asking Mr. Silent K. Do dinosaurs have nipples?"

"Stay focused," Ed answers.

"Mr. Silent K," Austin says. "Where do they get telephone pole seeds?"

"Stay focused."

Amy asks Tyasia how Mrs. Clanton will know when her baby is ready to come out.

"That's what the belly button is for. It pops out like a turkey, right Mr. Silent K?"

"Stay focused."

Not-Bob asks Austin, "How come all kangaroos have the same name?"

"No, they don't," Austin says.

"Yuh-huh. It's Joey. I saw it on TV."

"Hey, Mr. Silent K? Why do they say, 'dog years?' Do they have 'kangaroo years?'"

"Stay focused."

"Mr. Silent K," Logan asks. "Did you ever play 'I Spy' when you were a kid?"

"Yes. We used real spies."

"Huh?"

"Stay focused."

"Hey, Mr. Silent K," Jake says. "What's 'feces' mean?"

"Use it in a sentence."

"I just did!"

"Stay focused."

"Oh! Mr. Silent K," Amy exclaims. "My mother told me to tell my teachers I have my monthly. In case I need to go to the Girl's Room."

"Mr. Silent K," Andre says. "Do you have a lint-roller?"

"What!"

"A lint-roller. It's like tape but just the sticky part. My pants have dog hair on them."

"I know what it is. No, I don't have one. Stay focused."

Ed looks at the clock. *This is going to be a long day,* Ed thinks.

Ed stays after school and, still feeling stressed, writes down a list of everything going on. There are four classes of tests to correct; Larkin is living with him but so far so good; Derry's Improvement Plan assignment is due in a week; Savvy needs rabies shots and there's just not enough time to walk him every day; there's very little time to practice the song Heather Click is teaching him; he needs to make a decision on going to New York City for the Thanksgiving break or stay at home; there are two parents to call about behavior; report cards are due next week so all grades have to be in; and lesson plans have to be more detailed according to Derry. *So much for an easy job,* Ed thinks to himself and keeps writing his list. Duties of attending the championship football game, if the team makes it, is coming up; and monitoring his first detention is two weeks away. And spending time with his sister, a reason for moving here, is proving challenging as he had no idea she worked so many hours. Ed looks again at the half-page list and wonders if writing it all down was a good idea or not!

Ed calls Anita at home later that week.

"Hey, what are you doing Saturday night?"

"Are you asking your sister out on a date? I may be a widow but I'm not *that* desperate!"

"It's not a date, well I guess it is, kind of. Our school made the finals in football and—"

"I heard that. It's at our field because we have more bleachers. That's great."

"Right? And the game is this Saturday night. I have to be there for 'crowd control,' whatever that means. A bunch of teachers will be there."

"Sure. I'll go."

"But I need some help. I'm going to make some signs to encourage the players and students watching."

"Signs will be tough to see. How about using banners?"

"What kind of banners?"

"I've seen kids use sheets and paint slogans on them."

"That's a good idea. If I get the stuff will you help me make them Saturday afternoon? The game starts at 6:00."

"Sure. See you around two?"

"Great! Thanks, Sis."

Ed heads to the local 'Marge Has It' store since Walmart is thirty minutes away.

"I'm looking for some sheets," Ed says to the clerk.

"What color?"

"They have to be white ones. Oh, and pillowcases, too."

"What size?"

"Size?"

"What size is your bed?"

"Oh, no. These aren't for a bed. These are for a rally on Saturday night."

The clerk has stopped walking. "They're over there," she says briskly, changing her mood.

As she walks away, Ed gets it.

"No," he says. "They're for banners for the football game," but the aghast clerk is gone.

It's the Friday that Ed's 'My Country' is due. Ed works the room to look for quality reports that would qualify to be shared with the class. He sees 'Lego-Landia,' 'Puerto Andre,' 'Wizard Werewolf-Dom,' and 'Hey You-Topia.' *Oh boy*, he thinks to himself.

"OK," Ed says. "Time to share reports."

A hand goes up.

"Yes, Blake."

"Can I go first? I was done two weeks ago!"

Just then Ed's classroom door opens and Derry and Cutty walk in. Derry knew when the presentations were due because he constantly checked-in with Ed. But Cutty? Ed's first reaction is *Derry probably brought her to show off his idea, or to watch me fail.*

"Excuse me!" Derry says. "Good morning everyone. Principal Cutty and I heard you were doing some presentations today and we wanted to pop-in. I believe the topic is 'My Country.' Just ignore us and continue what you were doing."

The two find empty seats in the back of the room. Ed gets an idea.

"Yes, Blake. You can absolutely go first," Ed says, knowing it will be a quality presentation.

Blake is setting up the computer and the screen, then confidently begins.

"My country is an island," she states. "I named it Pangaea, after the single continent theory I'm *sure* you are all familiar with." She speaks with an air of superiority.

"The island's ecosystem contains components from all the current continents: sand from Africa; rocks from North America; plants from South America; and animals from all over, including koala bears from Australia."

Blake dazzles the room with her technological savvy that includes music, links to video clips, and exploding transitions.

"Every language is spoken and understood by everyone since they all came from the same place. They are the original citizens of Earth…"

The kids are actually applauding as Blake finishes ten minutes later. Blake is beaming.

"Very good," Ed says, sincerely impressed. "Very well done."

"Excellent work," Derry interjects, standing up. "Mr. Knudknickovich and I worked very hard on this idea. Ms. Cutty, would you like to say anything?"

"I certainly agree with Mr. Derry," Cutty says, obviously pleased. "And Mr. Knudknickovich—"

"That's Mr. Silent K," Jake interrupts. "His name is like sixty letters."

"I see," Cutty replies diplomatically. "Well, thank you all again for a wonderful job. We are off to visit other classrooms. Bye-bye."

Ed finally relaxes and feels an elusive sense of accomplishment. Ed asks for the next volunteer. Jake raises his hand. It's a sloppy drawing on a torn piece of cardboard. *Wait,* Ed thinks, looking closer. Is that a pizza box?

Andre jumps in. "Hey, Jake, did you make a window for your bedroom where you cut that piece out of your cardboard house?"

"Be nice!" Ed says, feeling *very* good that Blake went first.

Derry returns to Ed's room after school. The two speak amicably about the value of using projects versus lectures and note-taking. Ed genuinely thanks Derry but can't help wondering if the whole thing was a set-up to make the Vice Principal look good in front of Cutty.

Another of Ed's assigned duties is to host after school detention twice this school year. The first is this afternoon.

Derry walks into Ed's room.

"OK. Here's the list for detention. It's until five o'clock, and then you walk them up to the front doors so they can be picked up. At five. The list doesn't look too long."

"I don't know most of them," Ed says.

"It's a lot of seventh and eighth-graders. They're supposed to have work to do, but don't be surprised if they don't. The *good* teachers give them missing assignments to finish."

"Got it."

"OK. Now, I have to head out for something, but Cutty will be here. Take my radio and call her if you need to, but the expectation is that the teacher handles it."

"Got it."

"You have the list?"

"Got it."

"Spread them out as far as possible."

"Got it."

"Make sure you take attendance."

"Got it."

"Alright. I'm leaving."

"Good."

"What?"

"I said, 'Got it.'"

Students start to wander in. Most display disdain or a sullen attitude that makes it clear they don't want to be there. Mr. Silent K spreads them out.

"Alright," Ed starts. "Expectations. Do your work, no talking, no phones. Now, attendance. Ben. Ben?"

"That's him," a girl says, pointing.

"Isaiah. Isaiah?"

"That's him, over there," the same girl says.

"Andrew. Andrew?"

"He's in the back row. They're trying to be cool."

"Hey, Baker, why don't you shut up," one of the boys says.

Ed finishes attendance.

"OK," he says, curious. "What's everyone in for?"

The chatty girl whose last name is Baker says, "Andrew told Ms. Benz to F-off. Isaiah and Linda were kissing during gym class. Ben—"

"Baker! I swear you better shut-up!" Ben says. He starts to get up.

"Sit down," Ed says firmly. "Miss Baker, what are you in for?"

"Being a kiss-ass," Ben says.

"Stop!" Ed says.

"I was late to math three times and in eighth-grade that is automatic detention. But I was helping clean up in science, but Ms. Grey didn't care and said I was late. Do you have any work for me to do?"

"You're supposed to *have* work."

"It's all done. Ms. Benz lets me grade papers. Do you have any?"

"Hey Andrew," Ed says. "And you. Sit back down. Ben, right?"

"Tell him to stop looking at me or I'm going to pound him."

"What are you in for?" Ed asks Ben.

"Pounding him," he says, looking at Andrew.

Great, Ed is thinking. Two boys that fought are in the same room, *my* room.

The door opens and Mr. Spectre comes in.

"I have some work to pass out. Diamond Baker! What are you doing in detention?"

"Well…"

"Never mind. Ben, you owe me a short story. It was due last week."

"I don't have any paper," Ben replies.

"Here. I brought you some."

"I don't have a pencil."

"Here. I brought you one. I'll be back later."

It's quiet for about a minute. Ben is scrunching the paper.

Ben asks, "Can I listen to music on my phone?"

"No."

"But Mr. Spectre lets us as long as we are working."

Ed looks to Baker for a clue. She nods her head 'yes.'

"OK. Here's the deal," Ed says. "If you are doing your work, and as long as I can't see your earbuds or hear the music, you can listen."

"Do you have any work for me?" Baker asks again.

"Oh, that's right. Um, these are quizzes, fill in the blank. Here's the answer key and a red pen. Just put an X if it's wrong and write down how many they missed on the top."

It's quiet for about a minute.

"This one doesn't have a name on it."

"Just grade it anyway."

"This class is not very smart. There's a lot of red X's."

"Just grade, please. Quietly."

All is quiet. Ed decides to walk around to make sure everyone is working. He stops at Ben's desk. The paper is blank and crumpled. Ed sits down next to him.

"We had a deal. You're supposed to be writing a story."

Ben takes an earbud out. "I can't think of one."

"Well, do you have an idea for a plot?"

"No."

"Do you have some ideas about the characters?"

"No."

"Do you have any notes?"

"No."

"OK then," a frustrated Ed says. "This *is* going to be a short story."

"He's just playing dumb," Andrew says.

"Shut-up, Andrew."

"That's it! You're dead!"

Both boys get up. Ed has to stand between them.

"Sit down! Both of you!"

Ed gets the walkie-talkie and says, "Ms. Cutty?"

"Yes," comes a quick reply.

"This is Mr. Knudknickovich. I have the detention group. I have two boys who are trying to fight."

"Send one out into the hallway and I'll be right there."

"Andrew, go wait in the hall."

"Why should I go? He started it!"

"Just go!"

Andrew bumps Ben's chair as he goes by and Ben tries to kick him. Cutty arrives as Andrew opens the door to go to the hallway.

"Who's the other problem?" Cutty asks. "Ben?"

"He started it."

"Enough!" Cutty demands. "I'll take both of them with me. They should *never* be in the same room together! Sorry about that."

Thanks, Derry, Ed is thinking. He looks at the clock. It's only 3:30.

Thanksgiving week arrives, and teachers give 'thanks' for the Wednesday through Sunday break. Ed had thought about taking the train to New York to see friends but decides there is too much going on at home. Instead, he plans a small gathering at his house. Of course, Anita will be there, and Ed is sensitive to the fact that holidays for her tend to manifest melancholy over Harold's death.

George Larkin volunteers to cook and wakes early, whipping up all of the normal holiday dishes he used to help his late wife make. Guy White is coming over, and Ed invited all of the sixth-grade teachers, but some have other plans. Kilo stops by later in the day. Savvy gets a bowl of human food but still rotates between the kitchen and the dining room table, hoping for scraps. A good time is had by all.

The day turns into a great bonding session as stories are swapped. Anita talks about some of the issues she has faced in her high school so far this year and mentions that the 'Free Lunch Program' keeps expanding to more kids, meaning poverty in the county is on the rise.

Kilo talks about growing up in upstate New York, and how the snow reached his chest as a little kid. When he was older, he had to help his dad shovel snow off the roof! He also tells a few humorous stories about all his years teaching at Farmwood Middle School.

George tells stories about emigrating from Ireland as a child and trying to lose his accent. He goes on to talk briefly about his time in the army and then getting a college degree on the government's dime. No one brings up his current situation.

Ed entertains with stories about Jon Stewart and working on the show. He tells them that of course, he met many celebrities over the years, and his favorite all-time is Chelsea Handler, whom he admits he still has a crush on. He keeps talking but doesn't want to sound pompous about his former job. He also tells the group he is beginning to feel emotional attachments to many of the kids, especially Andre.

Guy is fairly quiet, giving a quick update on all his inventions, which so far have resulted in a big bag of nothing. He is the first to leave as he wants to get back to his family to watch the football games together.

As things wrap up, Kilo makes a toast. "To teachers," he says, "and the kids that we touch, er, I mean impact, despite the ongoing fight for more funds. Do more for less!" he exclaims sarcastically, repeating the School Board's mantra, then adds, "Here's to all we do." Glasses and beer bottles clink.

With everyone gone, and the kitchen put back together, George and Ed relax in front of the muted TV so they can watch the game but still talk.

"So, Eddie, is teaching what you thought it would be?"

"Well, Kilo is right. I had no idea of the bureaucracy in the education field. There is just so much 'stuff' we have to do that takes time away from the kids. It's like, maybe, when decisions are being made by the people in the School Board Office and the Department of Education, it would be nice if they asked, 'What does this do for the student?'"

Larkin is nodding his head. "I have definitely seen the change over the years, from increased parent apathy to a lack of respect for teachers. But I like your point: What does it do for the kids? We have to find every minute we can because every student has a story. Let me tell you two things I do. First, sometime during the first couple weeks of school, I go through all of my homeroom student's files. Oh, the stories, good and bad. But it helps explain everything from behavior, mental health, custody arrangements, and even abuse. And second, I don't know if you noticed, but I eat lunch a couple of days a week in the cafeteria so I can sit with the kids. I like to rotate around the table and have some one on one conversations. It's amazing what you hear, from 'we have five dogs' to a couple of boys talking about whose father is getting out of prison first. Some of it is a punch in the gut, and while I would never equate kids with dogs, they both want the same thing, attention and a comfortable atmosphere. School is a haven for many of them."

"Those are great ideas," Ed confirms. "I enjoy your passion after all of these years, and I hope I can emulate it. You're right. I see it every day, and that's why I can't understand some of the teacher's negativity and dream-busting rants to their students. Our role is to grow the tree, not chop it down."

"Well said!" It results in the final clink of beer bottles.

Chapter Thirteen

Kilo Jones, Principal Cutty, Mrs. Connors, who is the school system's lead council, plus several other school board officials are sitting at a large table in the school board office.

"You've got to be kidding," Kilo responds as to why he is there.

"I'm sorry, but I'm trying very hard not to laugh. OK. Can you explain that again?"

Mrs. Connors instructs the group to turn back to page two.

"Basically, you, and the school system, are being sued for educational malpractice."

"Is there such a thing?" Kilo asks.

"By a former student of yours, James Wagner. He is blaming us, you, for losing his job."

"I taught him like what, eight years ago? I didn't know there is a thing called 'Educational Malpractice.'"

"Unfortunately there is. There is some precedent. Now, Mr. Wagner claims he was arrested and fired from his job because of something you taught him in sixth-grade."

"What does he do?" Kilo asks. "Or what *did* he do?"

Mrs. Connors is up and walking around the room as she reads from her notes.

"He is, was, an HVAC specialist. The company he worked for at the time had maintenance contracts for several federal buildings in D.C. According to his statement, his crew was trying to check the airflow in the Capitol Building. There were complaints that it was too warm. He claims you told him natural gas has quote, 'no odor.'"

"That's true," Kilo answers.

"And," Connors continues, "the smell people associate with natural gas is an additive called 'mercaptan,' also a gas, but one that gives off an odor similar to rotten eggs."

"That's true," Kilo replies.

"So, Mr. Wagner, and this part is a little light on details, perhaps purposely, Mr. Wagner obtained this chemical in gas form—"

"Don't tell me," Kilo says.

"And sprayed it into the main system—"

"Don't tell me."

"So, he could more quickly tell, or smell, where the air was flowing and where it wasn't."

"In the Capitol building?" Kilo asks incredulously.

"Yes, which all of a sudden smells like gas or a gas leak, causing absolute panic. The whole place is going to blow!"

Everyone in the room is now laughing.

"The place is completely out of control. There was a debate in the Capitol building but luckily it wasn't full. But D.C. is shut down. The Capitol is evacuated. The Secret Service and Capitol Police are scrambling."

"When was this?" Kilo asks. "How come I never heard about it?"

"Apparently it was about three years ago. The Press was told it was a 'drill.' It made the national news, Congressmen and women are standing outside on the capitol steps in ninety-degree weather. Nobody looked very happy. You don't remember it?"

"Not really, but I'll definitely YouTube it when I get home."

The school board conference participants are still smiling or chuckling.

"Ridiculous or not," Mrs. Connors continues, "we have to respond. Mr. Wagner was fired, well arrested, and *then* fired. He hasn't worked in that field since. He can't pass a background check because he was flagged by the FBI."

"Is he on the 'No Fly List?'" Kilo jokes.

"Probably. But of course, he is the *victim* here. And naturally, he is *entitled* to compensation. Now I know we all find this humorous and frivolous, but we need to respond. Of course, negligence must be proven, as well as a clear detriment to a student's ability to learn."

"I don't think he had an I.E.P," Kilo responds.

Ms. Cutty, who has the student's file with her, flips through it.

"He did not," Cutty says. "He was not eligible for an Individual Education Plan, so we are safe there."

"Let me sum this up," Connors says. "The first case like this was actually in the seventies. It really evolved out of situations like kids with average intelligence being labeled 'retarded' by a teacher. This minimized their education, held them back, and there were no accommodations available at the time. So, there have been 'legitimate' concerns in the past. We will of course ask for a dismissal, but these things can take months, even years. Stay tuned. And because the FBI and Secret Service were involved, it's a federal issue. So, Mr. Jones, don't leave the country. Kidding."

The meeting ends and it is back to the everyday chore of teaching students.

A few days later Kilo has his students outside to work on a Solar System Project. The weather is nice for an early December day, but the kids are wearing light jackets or hoodies. They are using the school's softball field.

Kilo begins the instructions.

"OK. Everybody has the sheet of directions. You are working in teams of three. Each team should have ten flags. Home plate is the Sun. Yes?"

"There are only nine planets if you still include Pluto. Why do we have ten flags?"

"If you recall, you have to mark the Asteroid Belt as well. Now, start at the Sun, which is home plate, spread out to walk off the distances, and go in different directions. Walk the number of steps it says on your worksheet, plant the flag, and write down the name of the planet and stick that on each flag. The objective is to get a better idea of how large our Solar System is. Questions?"

"I'm cold."

"What flags? These things?"

"Why do I have to be in this group?"

"I have to go to the bathroom."

"What's home plate?"

"Can I sit down?"

"Can we go to the woods?"

"You know," a frustrated Kilo says. "In about ten seconds we are all going back inside. I told you to bring a jacket, and a pencil, and the instruction sheet. I told you these are the groups and I am not changing them. I also told you, and I'll say it one more time. Your behavior today determines if we ever go outside again. So, start figuring out who does what in your groups and get to work."

The kids start working. It is a challenge to watch the kids and answer their constant questions at the same time. Kilo has not yet notice that a couple students are missing.

Two kids have successfully made it into the woods without being seen, a difficult task since all of the tree's leaves have all fallen. Luckily there are plenty of bushes to hide behind.

Andre asks, "You got the matches, right?"

"No." Jake answers.

"What? Then why did we sneak down here, you moron?"

"Because I have a lighter, moron," Jake replies.

"Alright. We have to be quiet and we have to be quick, so keep your eyes and ears open. There's not a lot of wind but we oughta be able to get some kind of fire going and then beat it back to the field."

"What about houses?" Andre asks.

"What about them?"

"They won't burn too, will they?"

"Look how far away they are! Plus, they're on the other side of the creek! There are all these leaves and sticks in between. Besides, they'll be able to see it and call the Fire Department before it gets too big. We'll be gone by then!"

"Alright. Who's doing what?"

Jake answers. "Help me make a little pile of stuff to get started. Yeah, like that. Good. Now, you watch for anyone coming. If it's a kid just show 'em what'll happen if they tell." Jake pounds his right fist into his left hand and grins.

"Go ahead and light it," Andre says.

"OK. Are you watching?"

"Yeah. Why's it not doing nothing?"

"I'm trying," Jake says.

"Don't you have to blow on it? Mr. Jones is always saying fire needs oxygen."

"OK, OK!"

Jake is blowing so hard he gets dizzy and tries to stand up. The fire catches, but the hyperventilating Jake passes out, rolls down the hill and into the creek!

"Jake!"

Andre is just loud enough for Kilo Jones to hear him as he searches for his two missing students, his most *mischievous* students.

Kilo reacts quickly. "Blake, you're in charge. Keep everyone up here. Logan, do you have your phone?"

"Yes. Sorry, I forgot to put it in my lock—"

"Take it out, come over here, and film this. Quickly!"

Kilo Jones sees the smoke and gets to the fire fast enough to stomp it out. Logan is recording it on her phone. A soaked Jake is stumbling out of the creek. Andre is thinking about taking off into the woods. Blake can't stop the other students from running over to watch.

Kilo sees Andre and orders him and Jake up the hill to the field.

"You two sit here, and *don't move!* Everyone else go sit on the ground and be quiet. And I mean *quiet!*"

Jones uses the walkie-talkie teachers take outside in case of an emergency. Derry is on his way out.

When Derry gets there, he takes control. Kilo tells him it is taped on Logan's phone.

"I asked her to film it," Kilo says.

"Thank you. Our school resource officer is on the way. Logan, come with us, too. You're not in trouble; I need to see your phone, so follow us."

As Derry leads the small group toward the doors, the rest of the sitting science students squirm and try and whisper.

"Mr. Jones," Fowler says. "Is Andre in trouble?"

Ed and Kilo have gone to bat for Andre before. When the dust settles, Jake gets most of the blame because he had the lighter. Jake receives at-home detention for two weeks, the maximum penalty before getting sent to the 'alternative' school. Ed agrees to host Andre for after-school detention every day for two weeks. Ed plans to use the time to further mentor the boy whose father is not around. In addition, Ed figures he can use the time to help Andre with the material most likely to be on the state test for history. Also, Ed hopes this extra time and effort gets him points on his Improvement Plan.

Ed's plans for the first day with Andre is challenging.

"OK. Let's get started."

"We're going to have to do work?"

"Yes."

"Ah, man. That's not fair! Can I call Fowler and Logan?"

"No. What did you think we were going to be doing in after-school detention?"

"Eat pizza."

Ed has Andre stacking books and taping broken binders. They keep chatting.

"We have lots more work to do and then some studying," Ed tells Andre. "But maybe we can work out a quid-pro-quo for pizza."

"I'm not eating *that*. It sounds *disgusting!*"

"It's not food. It's Latin—"

"More Latin? Why is everyone always saying stuff in Latin? My grandma says we are Latino. Is that why?"

"Not exactly. Latin is a language; you know that. From a long time ago."

"You mean cavemen?"

"Not quite that far back."

"Oh. You mean before texting?" Andre asks.

"Sometime in between."

"So, what do teachers do in the summer?" Andre asks, randomly changing the subject like a typical kid.

"What do you mean?" Ed asks as the topic changes.

"Summer. When it's hot."

"I know what sum—"

"So, what do teachers do when they don't teach?"

"Well, it depends. Some get summer jobs."

"Like what?"

Andre has gotten up and is looking out the window.

"Well, I know Mr. White. Wait, no names. I know one teacher that drives for a limo company. Here, when you are done with those books, go back through them and look for swear words. Use this marker to black them out or erase it if it's in pencil."

"That'll take a year! Do teachers have to read books and stuff? Like, how do you know so much about history?"

"Mostly from college."

"I'm not going to college. I'm going to play in the NFL for the Ravens."

"That's a good goal but let me ask you this. Where do the NFL teams get their players?"

"Huh?"

"Where do they get their players?" Ed repeats.

"They draft them. I saw it on ESPN."

"Draft them from where?"

"From *college*. Gee, Mr. Silent K. You don't know— Oh."

"Yeah, 'oh.' So, you pretty much have to go to college and play football so the NFL can check you out."

"What do you have to do to be a teacher?"

"Go to college."

"Ah, man."

"You go to college and then you get your license."

"My grandma goes to the DMV for her license. I went with her."

"I'm talking about a *teaching* license."

"Wait. You got to have a license to be a teacher? Is there a test?"

Ed looks up from his stack of papers.

"Kind of. The tests are different based on—"

"But what are *you* going to do this summer?"

Ed decides to have some fun.

"Oh, um, I think I am going to start a Hobo Camp."

"My grandma doesn't like me saying that word."

"*Hobo* camp, to learn how to be a hobo."

"Oh. Wait. What's a hobo?"

"Well, you know, like a bum."

"My grandma says my dad's a bum."

"Um, well, this is different. See, a hobo doesn't have a job. They just kind of roam around the country, being lazy, sticking it to the man."

"You mean those people with shopping carts?"

"No. It would be too hard to use a shopping cart. See, they only own, or have, what they can carry. Let's start from the beginning."

Ed gets up and sits next to Andre.

"Geez," Ed says. "I can't believe I'm telling you this. OK, a hobo *looks* like a homeless person, kind of dirty, one set of clothes. But they *want* to be that way. They don't want a home. They put all their stuff in a bandana and tie it to a pole so they can carry it as they tour the country. So, at Hobo Camp, I'm going to help train them."

"Um, it's not that hard to look homeless."

"That's just part of it. I mean yes, I'll help them with the look and stuff. But there's so much more."

"Wait. Do you have to go to college to be a hobo?"

"No. As I was saying, you have to be able to make a fire in a barrel, but let's not talk about fire. You have to be able to open a can of beans with a rock, um, jump on and off a moving train, sleep on the ground, things like that."

"That's what I want to do! I want to be a hobo!"

"Oh, no, no, no. Don't say that. I'll probably get in trouble."

"What do they do for money?"

Andre is up and is rearranging things on Ed's desk.

"That's just it. They don't need money. They travel for free by hiding on freight trains, take baths in a river. It's a whole community. A whole lifestyle."

"No work and everything is free?"

"Well, it's not like Greece or anything, but close."

"I'm in! Please let me be a hobo!"

"Ugh. I should probably be more careful about what I say."

"But can I go to Hobo Camp with you?"

"I'll tell you what. It's our secret. I'll think about it."

"Hi, Mr. Derry."

"Hi, Andre. Mr. Knudknickovich, a word please."

Ed had no idea how long Derry had been there. Crap!

The next day, Nurse Atlas and Vice Principal Derry conspire again.

"He actually said 'Hobo Camp?'" Atlas asks.

"Yes. He is out of control."

"Then let me tell you an idea I have."

"Oh, boy. Close the door. What now?"

"You've seen that YouTube video Jones showed when Congress had to evacuate, right?"

"Of course."

"It made me think. Knudknickovich was a TV writer, right?"

"Yes. It's all in his file."

"Did he do any stand-up?"

"What do you mean?"

"Well, wouldn't you think the way to get hired writing jokes is to *tell* them?"

"I'm not following…"

"If he did some stand-up, then maybe someone recorded it, and if it's inappropriate—"

"And we can find it." Derry says excitedly.

"Then he can be terminated. It's still his first year!"

"Have you looked?"

"Not yet. Let's do it now. We somehow put the link on the school's website and then everyone can see it! Students and parents, everyone."

"Everyone," Derry echoes. "We find it, we post it, and good old social media does the rest. Start Googling!"

Chapter Fourteen

It is the Friday before Christmas break. Not only is this two-week vacation looked forward to since the first day of school, but it marks that the school year is almost half over. Ed and Anita have a trip to New York City planned since George can stay and take care of Savvy.

The mood in the teacher's lounge is jolly for a change.

"I started looking for a summer job already," Miss Vega says. "I'd love to be able to afford Wi-Fi."

"Anyone else?"

"I worked one summer at a high school in upstate New York," Kilo Jones chimes in.

"Teaching summer school?" Ms. Rivalry asks.

"No. I was in high school, and they would hire a couple of students every year to help spruce up the school during the summer. I mopped floors for a couple of weeks and then had 'gum duty.'"

Guy White asks, "What does that mean?"

"I had to flip over every desk, and chair, classroom by classroom, and scrape the gum off. That's 'gum duty.'"

"Eew! That's disgusting," Miss Vega says.

"It certainly was."

"What did they do with the gum?" Guy White asks.

"The gum? Why?"

"I'm just curious," Guy says.

Ed jumps in.

"Uh oh. Guy is scheming."

"We tossed it in the garbage can, obviously. They even made us wear gloves." Kilo says.

"Mm. That's too bad."

"How's that?" Kilo asks Guy.

"Well, all that gum…"

"Yeah, I could have probably made a mountain out of it."

"All that gum. What if, and I'm just thinking out loud," Guy replies.

"Uh oh," Ed says. "That's how it starts."

"I think there's an opportunity here. And Kilo, fifty-fifty partners to use that gum."

"For what?" Ed asks. "Chewed gum, by *kids* no less. That has got to be biohazard stuff, you know, in a red bag or box like they use for syringes."

"Not if you market it right," Guys says. "Let's see. Used again or comes back, maybe recycled. It comes from under the desk. Down under the—I've got it! 'Kangaroo Chew. The Gum from Down Under—the Desk!"

"That's disgusting," Miss Vega says, one of the few people paying attention.

"You might be onto something," Ed says as he rolls his eyes.

"Did anyone else see them haul Fowler out this morning?" asks Miss Vega.

"For what?" Ed asks.

"Well, from what I picked up from my students there was a group of boys in the gym locker room huddled around a phone. Apparently, it was Fowler's, and apparently, there were girlie pictures on it."

"You're kidding," Kilo says as the chatter in the room dies down. "Pictures of what?"

"Not *what*. *Who*. They're starting an investigation. They think it is a student's mother."

"Oh," Guy says. "That reminds me."

"That reminds you?"

"I have news. I received a call and a letter, certified, very official."

"And?" Ed asks.

"It was from PepsiCo, the Aquafina, and water division. They want to buy 'YURINE.'"

"What!" half the people in the room say.

"Sounds like you just won the lottery," Kilo says.

"Yes! They talked about maybe changing the name, but they are sold on the yellow color. But that's nothing. I have more buns in the oven. I'm working on a fish version of SPAM. I call it SPISH."

Lunch ends and the teachers trudge out to kill the last few hours before the Christmas break, always a hectic time.

Kilo and Ed meet in Kilo's classroom after school. Andre has finished his two weeks of detention. Ed actually enjoyed the time and feels a sense of accomplishment that he is starting to be a good influence on him. He feels very close to the youngster after getting to know him better. His grandmother confirmed it one day when she picked him up at five o'clock. She even mentioned Andre seems to be maturing a little under Ed's guidance.

Veronica Vega tentatively comes in and closes the door.

"Hey, Verny," Kilo says. "We're just telling stories before we leave for break."

"Can I talk to you guys for a minute?"

"Sure! Sit down. Do you want us both in here?"

"Yes. I respect both of you and, well. I might have fudged my application a little bit. This is all hush-hush."

"Sure," Ed says. "Everyone does it. I'm actually a robot!"

"And I never went to college," Kilo says, not understanding the gravity of the situation.

"Uh oh. You're not laughing. What did you do?"

"Well, I'm not supposed to be here."

"At this school?"

Kilo interjects. "I think I know what you are saying."

"I'm not supposed to be *here*. My work visa kind of expires next month. I didn't disclose this when I was hired. This is my future we are talking about. My whole life! I'm not sure—"

The classroom door opens and Cutty walks in.

"Oh! I didn't know you were having a meeting. I just want to remind everyone again to turn off and unplug everything since the building will be closed for two weeks. I'll leave you alone."

"It's OK," Kilo says. "We're just telling war stories."

"That sounds like fun. Oh, really quick. I do have something to talk to Kilo about."

"No problem, we can leave," Ed says.

Cutty continues. "That's not necessary. Everyone will find out eventually. You know what I say, 'the only secret in this building is a thought that hasn't happened yet.' It's about the lawsuit. I just got an update from Mrs. Connors at the School Board Office about the quote 'Malpractice suit.'"

"They tossed it?" Kilo says, smiling.

"No. Unfortunately, a Grand Jury passed it through. We are going to trial."

"You're kidding!" Kilo exclaims.

"I wish I were. This will be a major distraction for everybody and talk about a waste of time."

"But Kilo's covered, right?" Ed asks.

"Yes. To a point. Mrs. Connors still isn't particularly concerned yet, although she wishes it had been thrown out, and quietly. Now it will probably make the newspaper. Nonetheless, I hope you all have a great break. I'm going to check the other classrooms." Cutty leaves.

Verny Vega hangs out in the room. With no plans for the break, she is not in a hurry to leave.

Ed's phone vibrates. It's a text from Heather Click. The two have become good friends. Ed figures she wants to change the day for the next guitar lesson, so he just glances at it quickly, and finds a pleasant surprise. 'Hope this isn't too forward. Stay for dinner after the next lesson?'

Ed, Verny, and Kilo keep chatting.

"What a weird first half, you two."

"This isn't normal?" Ed asks.

"I see more crazy stuff every day," Verny adds.

"I'm talking about the big stuff. A homeless Larkin. Jake suspended. Keeping Andre out of trouble. Verny's immigration issue. Guy selling his invention. Fowler in some kind of phone trouble. And I heard a student brought a BB Gun into Anita's high school today."

"Yeah," Ed adds. "And I'm supposed to make sure Andre passes all of his classes the rest of the year. And all of his state tests."

"That's going to be tough for math. He is really struggling," Verny states. "I hope he does better in the second half. He's going to need some tutoring."

"Ugh, the second half," Kilo bemoans. "State testing. You have no idea how time-consuming this is. And January is when the administration makes personnel decisions for next year, including if new teachers get to come back."

"Great," Ed says. "When will I know? I'm actually feeling pretty confident, now that I have a routine down and I've gotten to know the kids better. My goal is to get off probation and return next year."

"Mine, too," adds Vega.

"They usually make the decision next month," Kilo says. "I haven't heard anything bad. I think you both should feel good about the first half, except something about an old video of you, Ed."

"I don't know about that."

"Good! Don't worry about it until after the break."

"I do know Derry doesn't like me. And neither does Atlas."

"Yeah, and we have to help you, Verny. I might know someone."

"And you have that silly lawsuit," Ed says. "Larkin still needs a permanent home and I have to get invited back next year. I better! I don't even want to *think* that this could all end after one year."

Principal Cutty opens the door, out of breath.

"I need your help! Larkin is having a heart attack."

The three scurry to George's room. Cutty, still on the phone with 911, props open the nearest side door for the ambulance in route. Atlas grabs the closest defibrillator and is hurrying to the room. Chaos!

www.ingramcontent.com/pod-product-compliance
Lightning Source LLC
Chambersburg PA
CBHW061731050726
47598CB00002B/440